LARK

DARK DUET

PART ONE

EMMA COLE

Reviews
Please do consider leaving a review as it helps others
determine if this is the right book for them. In addition to that,
the more interest there is in a particular series, the more likely
that it will get bumped up in the schedule. (If we don't know
how you feel about a book/series, we don't know what you'd
like to see next.)

Pirating
Please don't be a pirate.
It really does have an impact.
It is theft, so don't do it!

BLURB

Dark. Gritty. Taboo.

Broken-hearted and mortified after being dumped when she expected a proposal, Lark calls her best friend and roommate for a rescue. While waiting to be picked up, she ducks around the corner into the alley to gain her composure, unaware it will be the action that leads her into a trafficking syndicate.

Kidnapped, along with her best friend, Lark wakes up to find herself in a cell with her friend, her ex, and her exes' partner where they are forced to submit or become casualties of circumstance. They must stick together and comply—making the best they can out of a terrible situation, to survive.

Stripped of all dignity and choice will Lark make it out alive? If she does, what will be left of her?

Dedicated to all the dirty birdies!

PURGATORY

Disbelief courses through my body as I sit in my favorite café. Mid motion of dipping my biscotti into my coffee cup, my hand hangs suspended as I glare at my long-term boyfriend, Rex. He looks pained yet resolute. As if *he's* not the one that just told *me*, in public—obviously to minimize the meltdown— that he loves me, but he has issues he needs to work out. That it's not fair to make me deal with them and if I'm still willing once he works them out, he'll tell me about them and hopefully, we can get back together. Well, he said it in a lot more detail than that, but that's pretty much what I got from it. The old 'it's not you, it's me' routine. I'd met him here tonight, tentatively expecting a proposal, and instead got dumped.

I know that something has been bothering him lately and that it started when his childhood friend came to visit and then abruptly took off without a word or his belongings a couple months ago. Obviously, now I know more than just his absent friend has been on his mind. Unsure how I could have missed something as big as him wanting to end things, I stare at his handsome face. The shock begins to turn to anger, bringing on the urge to punch those perfect white teeth. *Years,* I've wasted on the d-bag.

Objectively, I realize that even while wanting to deck him, he's still attractive to me. His blond hair is buzzed short on the sides, a little longer on the top. He's fresh-shaven, making his dark blue eyes more prominent than usual. I want to blacken them both. I'm frozen, speechless, trying to process everything he's just said.

He leans in to kiss me after gathering his things up and telling me he'll see me around. Right, like that's going to happen. Leaning back, I refuse to acknowledge his hurt look; I'm sitting here with a mouthful of biscuit that I can't swallow because the lump in my throat is threatening to choke me if I attempt it. I see Emmett, Rex's investigative reporter partner and best friend, waiting on the sidewalk through the window. He looks anxious and a little sketchy. And hot. Unfortunately, the hotness is outdone by the sketchiness. Guy is weird.

He's got an angel's face that draws looks from men and women alike, crystalline blue eyes framed by lashes darker than the light blond hair on his head that's currently shaved in textured lines on the back and sides with a shock of long sun-bleached locks in a wedge overhanging his face. He reminds me of an anime character or one of the main characters from a fantasy video game. Like I said, seriously fucking hot.

Something is going on with them, but as my heart has just been ripped through my ribcage, in public no less, I'm not apt to try to figure it out right now. It's all I can do to not scream obscenities at Rex. I can't believe he brought his partner with him for this, even if we were all friends. Well, as part of the break-up rules, I'd imagine he's no longer going to be a friend of mine.

Trying to gather my composure, I watch them through the window as they meet up outside, exchanging words before they walk out of my line of sight. I get my phone out to text my best friend and roommate, Braeden. I instantly get a text back telling me what a douche my now ex-boyfriend is, and that he'll be here in ten minutes. Profusely thanking my past self right now for not moving in with Rex and Emmett months ago when Rex had asked, I gather my things and walk outside, going around the building to the mouth of the alley, not wanting anyone to see me if I lose my composure before I get home with Braeden. They have a mammoth-sized modern cabin in the woods. I'd been tempted but liked living with Braeden. Rex always accused him of being secretly in love with me, even though he most definitely would have preferred Rex if he were to choose between the two of us. *Not exactly sporting the preferred equipment.* Even so, Rex never believed me, and that had caused a bit of a strain where my best friend was concerned.

Braeden is six two, two hundred thirtyish pounds of muscle. He religiously works out as a personal trainer and self-defense instructor. We go running several times a week and work out just as often together. He's Italian/Greek with midnight hair, swarthy complexion, and refined features. If that isn't enough, the brightness of his sea-green eyes pops in all that gorgeousness, hinting at more than the primary ethnic-ities he claims. I can see why Rex would be worried, but he's my best friend and has been since he was an exchange student our senior year. My parents adopted him when his grandpar-ents passed while he was here in the States. So *technically,* he's my adopted brother, but neither of us acknowledge that other than legally. We moved in together during college and have been inseparable since.

I see Braeden getting out of his car down the block where he parked and send him a quick text telling him where I am. As soon as I send it, I hear a muffled scuffle and grunts. Going a little further down the alley, I peer around a dumpster. Dark silhouettes appear in the low light filtering from a streetlamp at the opposite end. After a moment my eyes adjust, bringing into focus men fighting. I briefly debate running back to the cafe for help before Braeden comes around the corner, headed toward me. At my frantic motioning, he notices the scuffle going on. Shaking his head, he's reaching for my arm, presumably to pull me away, when I hear the voice that just left me yelling at the other men.

"Rex!" I know it's him. Even after what happened a few minutes ago, I can't *not* try to help him. "Braeden, call the cops!" I take off for the struggling figures with Braeden right behind, whisper yelling at me to stop. A moment before I reach the group, I notice Emmett is unconscious on the ground, and his hands and feet are bound together. Looking further back to Rex, his expression turns to one of horror as he makes eye contact with me, and the hesitation is enough for one of the attackers to sink a needle into his neck. An abrupt "NO!" is all he gets out before he crumples to the ground. I turn to run when the men who are in masks and gloves turn toward me. Braeden catches up to me at the same time, trying to pull us both back to safety. I feel the prick of a needle in my neck from behind and a burn of the fluid as it's being injected. The world starts to go fuzzy as I see Braeden receive the same treatment; everything goes black.

2
A LIE ON TOP OF A LIE

"**S**he shouldn't have been anywhere near us when it went down," are the first words I hear whispered as I drift back to consciousness, but I can't place the voice right off. I'm still too fuzzy-headed. I know something's wrong, *really* wrong. It's just not coming back yet.

"What the fuck are we going to do now? They took both of them. I can't concentrate on this with them here. *We* were warned how bad it was going to be, but *she* didn't sign up for this. Neither of them did."

"We have to tell them. If our cover is blown, we'll all be killed, and so will anyone else they think is involved." *What the hell are they talking about?* My head hurts, and my mouth feels like it's been stuffed with cotton balls. I hear a pained moan, realizing there's a third person near me. I try to force my eyes open to see where I am. Turning my head, I manage to get them to open up a little, and the light hurts my eyes. As they adjust, I realize there isn't much illumination, but it's enough to make the little dwarves that have taken up residence in my head increase their mining efforts on my brain.

As my focus comes in, it registers that I'm on a concrete

floor, and it's cold. My head is resting on something cushy, and I'm covered with something that feels like fabric, I'm guessing a blanket. I take in concrete walls, no windows, and three men. Rex, Emmett, and Braeden. Braeden is the one moaning, lying not far from me. Rex and Emmett are sitting up against the walls across from me, still zip tied. I realize then that I'm also bound. This instantly pisses me off, and as what I heard when I first woke up begins to register, my fury increases.

"Are you telling me you know how I ended up here?" My voice is rusty and weak, yet I still manage to convey my scorn for the two men propped on the wall. "Someone better start explaining." As I try to sit up, I realize my head is laying on bundled up fabric, and I'm covered in an old flannel shirt. I'm thankful, but it doesn't do a thing for the anger coursing through my veins. As soon as I regain my equilibrium, I'm going to kick some serious ass.

"Lark, baby..."

"Don't fucking 'baby' me, Rex. You said we were over."

"Lark, I'm sorry. *This* is why. I had to. I didn't want to chance you being involved with this." He looks nervously at the door like he's waiting for someone to walk in. Based on our treatment so far, I don't doubt that it's not going to be a good thing.

"Explain. Now."

"Yeah, someone tell me why in the big blue sky I am tied up in a cell." Braeden's voice comes out, low and raspy. I start scooting over on my bottom in an awkward crab crawl across the floor to check on him.

Rex sighs. "I'm going to be blunt here. We don't have long before we're monitored. Lark, Braeden, I'm so, so sorry you got caught up in this. Emmett and I are actually undercover agents. Being investigative reporters is our cover." He winces at my surprised inhale. He knows he's fucked up and not just from the sharp glare I affix to replace the betrayal I know was written all over my face a moment ago. He continues his explanation. "We were supposed to be 'kidnapped' in three days as part of our new assignment. Only it's way too early, and now you've both been pulled in too." Rex pauses and closes his eyes. Very quietly, so I can hardly hear, he says the next part, "They're a human trafficking ring that deals in the sex trade. The victims get kidnapped, trained, and then sold at auction every six months. I stumbled onto it after Donnie took off; it wasn't willingly. Emmett and I were supposed to get as much intel as we could and then the agency we work for would 'buy' us. Frankly, I still shouldn't tell you all this, but since you're here, too, I just don't see a way to get you out without most likely getting you killed. Baby, I'm sorry, but if you want to get out alive, you're going to have to play along." I hear a sharp intake of air from Braeden. *Yeah, buddy, I feel the same way. I don't think I can make it a day, let alone have to continue to be a kidnappee for six months until I can get sprung.*

"Rex, are you telling me that if I don't cooperate with being trained as a sex slave, I'll be killed? You're fucking insane if you think I'm not going to fight that shit, and you know it. I'll keep my mouth shut about what you're here for, but I will remove the balls from any asshole that tries to touch me. I'm not keen on being murdered, but I'm also sure as fuck not sitting there and taking it like a goddamned whore." I'm yelling now, and all three men are shushing me. Maybe I shouldn't be so loud, but this shit is *not* happening. I want off the boat and I want off now.

I return my attention to Braeden, noting that he looks okay for the most part, just a little bruised up. "You okay, Brade?"

"Yeah, I think so. Really sore, might have some nasty bruises come morning." Braeden pauses to take a breath. "So, you two were going undercover to infiltrate a sex and human trafficking ring and somehow managed to get the two of *us* kidnapped with you? Am I following, correctly?" His voice has turned dark and angry.

"It wasn't on purpose, dude. Rex, I told you to take care of this earlier. If you had, they wouldn't be here." Emmett is just so sensitive. What an ass. Wait, he was saying something earlier about this, that means…

"You were just breaking up with me for this? Really, you couldn't have just said, 'Hey Lark, I'm gonna go fuck some people for my job, I'll let you know when I'm back in town?' I would have been pissed, sure, but you didn't need to make me think I did something wrong, you ass!" I know I'm not making much sense as I hear the words come out of my mouth and still want to smack him, instead I turn to Braeden.

"Hey Brade? You think we should be proper kidnapped slaves, or try our luck at trading these two?" Holding up my hand, I silence the two in question as they begin to object. I love Rex, and I care about Emmett to a point. This doesn't change that, but I'm pissed. They could have handled it differently.

"Honey, I think we'd all be killed. I think for now, we resist where we can and make a good show out of it. Just don't push anyone to hurt you. I don't think I could stop myself from retaliating." Braeden looks resigned.

"Umm…sex slaves. Since this is your gig, do you know who I'm going to be forced to fuck?" My words as well as my gaze are venomous and directed at both Rex and Emmett. I'm still not believing this shit. I'm waiting on someone to jump out from a reality show.

Rex rubs the back of his neck. "See, about that— we were entering as a pair already selected out for a lady that runs the Eastern Europe branch of this. We were— well, um—Lark, I'm pretty sure Emmett and I were designated as a pair intended to fuck each other, and I'd imagine a woman would have been tossed in for 'training' as needed." Rex closes his eyes with the last part. He *should* be ashamed of himself. Taking the assignment in the first place and breaking up with me over it. I can see where I rate. Directly below his job and partner.

Emmett pipes in. "Only way I see to salvage this is for our contact, who is also supposed to be our trainer along with his assistant, to add you two to the equation. And Lark, this isn't our usual type of gig. Most times we're more of a get in, get out, no hanky-panky nonsense. Rex thought he was doing you a solid by not cheating." Emmett is direct and to the point. And not a bit repentant about it from the tone of his voice. Sketchy asshole. Thinking about the scenario, I flush from my chest to the roots of my hair and bury my face in my hands with a groan.

"This is not happening. I'm never dating again." I look up, and my gaze touches on each one of them. "I'm going to be fucking you all, and you're all going to be fucking each other and possibly two others. You guys are nuts." I'm incredulous that this is happening, and about two seconds from freaking the fuck out.

"That about sums it up. I'm sorry, baby. I never meant for you to even have a chance at this touching you. I love you." I stare at Rex. I still love him too, but I'm not about to say it right now. Instead, I flip him off and ignore him, choosing to speak to my bestie instead.

"Brade, sweetie, I'm sorry, but you're going to have to figure out how to get it up for me. Better you than some gross stranger, anyway." He rolls his eyes at me.

"Thanks, honey, glad to know I rate right above perverted men," Braeden says dryly, recognizing my lame attempt at levity well enough to not be hurt.

Turning a glare on the other two, I demand, "Which one of you is done and ready to fess up?" Neither answers me. "Fuck." It's not a joke.

Still speaking to him and ignoring the others, I ask, "So, you with me on this?" I'm not gonna lie. I'm nervous and scared as all get out. If I think about it too much, I might have a panic attack. In this room, I'm scared, but I know I'll be *terrified* once something actually happens. Right now I'm trying to keep it together the best I can. *Fake it 'til you make it is a thing for a reason, right?*

"You know I'm with you all the way, honey. Never going to let anything separate us." He's hugging me with his body the best he can, and I take some small comfort in it. As I think about it, I realize it really doesn't matter how I ended up here. Even if it wasn't Rex and Emmett's fault, it still could have happened; shitty things happen on the daily in the news. I hear the scuff of shoes outside the door and a beep, then the lock disengaging as my breathing gets shallow. I have no control over what happens to me from here, and I know it. *I'll eventually get free, but what will be left of me when I do?*

3

SHIT GETS REAL

A tall man walks in with another of a more average height behind him. Auburn hair and brown eyes on the first. Those eyes are hard when they encompass the room, then light up with surprise and maybe a hint of concern when they land on me and Braeden. He immediately turns a dark look on Rex and Emmett, and I get the feeling that this must be their contact, and things are already not going according to plan.

"What the fuck," comes from the shorter man, confirming my thought. Dark brown curls and, from what I can tell in the dim light, either light blue eyes or maybe gray. The look of surprise on his face as he turns to the other man makes me think he's in on this too.

So glad everyone else was in the know. Might have been nice to have been forewarned to drop my boyfriend like a hot rock as soon as this little plan was hatched. It's still surreal that I'm in this type of situation, and honestly, I think I'm in shock.

More footsteps sound, and both men don expressionless masks. The men coming in are big, and there are many. I'm thinking our escorts have arrived. They separate and pull us up one by one. I'm trembling and begin to freak out when they pull me away from Braeden. Quickly and quietly, before I start to struggle, he says, "Honey, just cooperate for now. Save it for when you need it."

I really think this constitutes as needing it. I must silently convey it well enough with my mutinous look because he gets uncharacteristically sharp with me. "Lark, shut up and cooperate. We'll fix whatever later. You have to stay alive. Understand?" I nod, and his eyes soften. Quietly, he whispers, "Love you, bird brain."

"Who authorized the extras?" This from the tallest man that led the others in.

One of the other guards watching us closely, answers him. "They interrupted our acquisition, so I decided to bring them here. They are young and attractive, maybe a little sport for us guards if you don't want them, too?" The man is seriously disgusting, and from his speech and accent, English isn't his first language. Licking his lips as he stares at me, tied and hunched over in the grip of another guard, his eyes are flat and emotionless. Other than the shark-like curve to his mouth at the suggestion of us being his prey, that is.

My stomach churns as I pray to any god, demon, angel, or wannabe superhero that I won't be given to him, and do my best to stop my trembling hands, so as not to look so breakable.

"It causes me to adjust my plans, and I'm not happy to have to do that." Without even looking at the man, he snaps his fingers and gestures behind him. Three others walk in, and now it's getting very crowded in here. "Men, since you needed a new toy so badly, take this one here. Maybe this will remind you to follow my instructions in the future."

Immediately, the guard goes on the offensive, but he is encompassed by men that are all relatively his same size. He's pissed, yet they overpower him easily. I can't imagine he's going to live long after they're done with him.

Our guards file out leaving the two newcomers and us prisoners. The man in charge looks from me to Rex.

"Am I to understand that you explained things to these two?" His eyebrow is arched up with an expectant look as he waits.

"As much as possible, yes. No details, just the gist of it." Rex won't meet my gaze when I look at him. Can't say I blame him, as I badly want to hit him.

Addressing all of us, he shares, "My name is Apollo Vitti. You may call me sir or master from here on out. I am not from your law enforcement, as your men here are. They should have explained, so do not expect me to act in such a manner. It also would not do well for you to address me informally. I can direct things to a point. Anything catching attention will be dealt with immediately as I cannot have anyone suspect what is happening. I truly apologize that you were both pulled into this situation, but I cannot offer kindness from this point on without raising suspicion." Turning to the other man, his dark eyes shutter. "Please take the new acquisitions to begin the intake process." Turning on his heel he exits the room leaving us with his companion.

As the one left comes closer, I see his eyes are gray. He looks kindly at me with a touch of sadness. How did someone with such empathy end up in his position here? He cuts our bindings, and Braeden instantly comes to wrap his arms around me, my back to his front. I lean back into him, smelling his spicy aftershave that he loves so much. That small normality makes me feel more grounded. The man glances at Brade's arms around me with a bit of surprise after glancing at Rex.

"My name is Marcus. You can call me that in private, but make sure it's 'sir' in front of others. It is safe to call everyone sir or madam. Only Apollo will be master. Do not call anyone else that, it will create problems you don't want, I can assure you." He opens the door and gestures for guards to come in. "I will be escorting you to the intake wing. Do not try anything, just follow. I do not wish to damage you." This last is addressed to us as he walks out of the room.

We're led down a corridor with track lighting and gray painted walls and floor, all concrete. I'm starting to think we're in some kind of underground compound. We hang a left as we come to a split, before continuing on. The hallway has doors every so often, and some of the rooms that stand open have medical equipment. Much like a hospital, there is an antiseptic smell. I don't hear any sounds either, other than our footsteps and the rush of air through the ducts above us. I come to a sudden stop as a guard grabs my arm. Gripping Braeden's hand tightly, I pull him with me, trying to dislodge myself from the guard.

"This is your stop, girly, stop fighting me." *That's not likely to happen. I refuse to be separated.* Marcus comes around and grabs my arm that is holding Braeden's, while two other guards step in to grab his upper arms.

"You all have a process to go through. This will happen one way or another." This comes from Marcus, as the door behind him opens up. I see that it's an examination room, and I turn my gaze on Rex. Anguish and hate war for dominance in me, and I see him visibly flinch. This is his fault, and he knows it. Emmett looks pissed when I glance at him, and Braeden is sad and trembling with the need to struggle. I lift my chin and give him my best determined look. Let them get out of sight so I don't have to worry about them getting injured on my behalf, then I'm kicking the first person to touch me.

I turn to step into the room with my escorts as Marcus leads the others away. Upon entering, I take note of the exam room table and supplies. The door is shut, and two guards remain with me. The room is large and has another door at the other side that opens as I pull myself to a halt. I'm not moving a step further without an explanation. Yet another man walks in, this one in a white lab coat with the usual stethoscope around his neck. How can a doctor work for a place like this? He doesn't look malicious, but I don't think I'm going to get too far with sympathy either. As if reading my thoughts, he speaks.

"Don't appeal to me to help you escape. I cannot help you. Please sit on the table." I look from one male to the next until I've eyed each of them, making sure they aren't trying any funny business. Sitting on the table doesn't seem too harmful, so I comply. "First, I'm going to do a routine physical, and then I have questions for you. After those questions, we will conclude the second part of the physical." Well, he's certainly straightforward. "I'm going to start now, please remain still and follow my directions. I am Dr. Brent Martins. You may call me Dr. Brent or Dr. Martins. What is your name?"

"Lark."

"Last name?"

"Jones."

"Really?"

"Yes, *really*." *Idiot*. He doesn't remark on anything else.

He goes through the usual, blood pressure, temperature, listening to my lungs and checking reflexes. I use the opportunity to scan him. He's shorter than the other men, but seems fit. Dark blue eyes and light brown hair. A bit of a shadow of a beard, as if he hadn't shaved today, covers a square jaw. He's not unattractive, yet his eyes are mostly blank, and his movements methodical. I get a little concerned when he has me lay back, but it's just to palpate my stomach area, and I am directly sat back up. This is way too easy, and I'm waiting for the other shoe to drop. He pulls out a blood draw kit from a drawer. I cross my arms mutinously.

"I need to take some samples to test for any illnesses and evaluate your general health. Please hold out your arm."

"No. I'm done with this. You had your exam. You don't need my blood."

"Lark, you are not in a spa or on vacation. I'm certain you are aware that this is now your life. Resign yourself quickly. All acquisitions are screened before training, and I will also be giving you regular checkups during your training or when you receive injury." *When* I receive injury, not *if*. This man is dispassionate, as if he were commenting on the weather instead of commenting on my impending brokenness. I feel another surge of anger rush through me, followed by helplessness as my arm is grabbed by a guard while the other holds my body. They took me by surprise before I even thought to fight. I'm going to have to be more alert. This is the second time I was taken unaware.

I kick out at the doctor and am forced down as an arm swings out from the exam table and straps appear. They quickly secure me with my arm out. Glaring at the doctor the entire time he takes my blood, I kick myself again for thinking the table looked safe enough to sit on. The table is sat up after at least six little vials are filled. That's enough to make me lightheaded since I'm pretty sure it's been almost a full day since I ate. I can't be sure without knowing the time, but I'm definitely beyond hungry.

The doctor must notice my situation and hands me a glass of orange juice after releasing my arm. I desperately want it, but after everything else, I'm afraid it's drugged. With exasperation, the doctor takes a drink, draining a quarter of the glass before offering it again. I guess that's good enough. I warily take it, and though I want to drain it, I sip at it instead.

"Do you see that your cooperation will be ensured one way or another? Now, time for the questions. How old are you?"

"Twenty-seven."

"Have you ever been pregnant?"

"That's not your business." Yeah, so not answering personal

questions. Name, birthday, ect. They can get that from my purse since I'm sure they have it. My driver's license will tell them that I'm brown-eyed, brown-haired, even if it's more a dark brunette bordering on black, and just about an average weight for my five and a half foot self. The rest they can forget.

"I need to know the answers to these questions. Your sexual health is going to be very important to you, very soon." Again, with the 'I couldn't care less' tone. What is wrong with this man?

"Again, I'm not discussing it. Not your business."

"Let's continue, then. We'll come back to that. How many sexual partners have you had?"

"Are you dense? I'm not answering your questions. *It's not your business.*"

He continues with his questions as I continue to refuse to answer. Have you had any STD's, are you on birth control, do you take regular medications, have you had any injury or surgery to your pelvic area or reproductive organs. The latest, have you had anal sex or multiple partners at one time, makes me worry, yet I answer the same to it all.

"Your refusal to answer isn't going to help you, and as I see that you are going to be uncooperative, I will give you one chance to undress and put this gown on or the guards will strip you; that is how you will remain until my exam is finished." Well, finally I get a reaction. Not a good one, but it's something. I contemplate it. "If you agree to cooperate, I will have the guards stand in the hall for this portion. Your dignity will not remain intact forever, but for now, I can grant you this." Maybe he's not completely unfazed. Maybe I can work with this after all. The guards make noises as if to argue against it, but he just glares them into submission.

"I'll cooperate." I say it quickly and hope I won't regret this.

"Very well, you two, wait outside unless I call. I have my call button in case I need assistance." The guards grumpily leave the room, almost seeming disappointed. Disgusting fuckers.

"I'm not leaving or turning my back on you, put the gown on." He releases my bonds before handing me the usual exam gown and begins putting tools on a tray next to the table. I can't see what he has around the raised back of it. He's not directly looking at me, so I tie the gown on over my clothes, then quickly shimmy out from under them while staying covered. When I turn back around, I see the doctor trying to suppress a smile. "I can't say I've quite seen a patient change that way before."

"I'm not really a patient though, am I? More of a captive." He nods his head, and I think I briefly see regret in his eyes before they blank again.

"Please get up on the table." He gives me the standard little square blanket that falsely gives a person a sense of being covered up. I scoot up onto a little blue pad after the table has been laid flat again. Out come the stirrups, and I put my stockinged feet in them. *Yes, I left my socks on. It's not exactly warm in here.* "We'll start at the top and work our way down." Knowing the drill, I put my arms up, and he proceeds with the breast exam, asking questions here and there, noting that I'm a C-cup before finishing the area. Working his way down, he's examining my lower abdomen right above my pubic line when he notices my curiosity. "Looking for c-section scars."

"No, I haven't been pregnant as far as I know." I don't want to give anything up, but I also don't want to be minutely examined either.

"Feel like answering any more questions?" I snort, and that's answer enough. Sighing, he moves between my legs. "Scoot down some, I'm sure you've done this before." I comply and immediately feel gloved hands examining my pelvic area.

"When did you decide to get your jollies off by becoming a doctor for a sex trafficking ring?" I'm watching him intently while I make my accusation. He doesn't disappoint when he pales and jerks his hands away. He recovers quickly, glaring at me and handling me a tad rougher than before with his inspection. He pulls my nether lips apart, examining them for what, I don't know. Maybe warts? I think that's a thing. When he manipulates my clit, I jump, cheeks burning in embarrassment. I want to put my legs together, and my knees start to drift closed.

"Please keep them open."

I hear a click of a lid and then feel a cool wetness that makes me jump again. Fingers enter me, and the doctor proceeds with the internal portion of the pelvic exam. I'm used to women with smaller hands. This man's hands aren't small, and he's feeling out every nook and cranny. His fingers push in, reaching as his other hand presses down on the outside. I grimace and make a sound of pain. He immediately looks up at me and does it again. "Does that hurt when I push?"

"No shit, asshole," I yell at him, bringing my knees together instantly to dislodge his hand.

"Does it normally hurt when you get a pelvic exam?" To avoid any more of the pushing, I share enough to satisfy him.

"Yes and no. My gyno tells me I'm more sensitive than others, but that's not totally uncommon. Mostly, I think it's the size difference. Most men don't go digging around and pushing on things with their bigger hands." He looks surprised for a moment and also concerned. *How many women has he examined like this?*

"I don't specialize in this field, but I assure you I am fully trained. I was brought in for you as a special case. I apologize if I was too rough." He looks angry, but I don't get the feeling it's directed at me. "I'll try to be more careful as I proceed."

Knowing I'm not getting out of it, I relax my legs out again and feel the cold, odd shape of the speculum enter me. After getting it situated, he clicks it open and starts the scraping.

Again, I tense and hiss at the sting. I hate these exams, they always hurt. I see the doctor shake his head. He removes everything, considerately cleaning me up. "I apologize in advance." I feel a cold liquid at my anus and tense. "Have you ever been penetrated anally?" Of course now I have to answer. Maybe he won't if I haven't.

"No."

"I'll be as careful as I can." Before I can protest, he slides a gloved finger in. I'm so shocked at first that I don't move. After that, I recognize the pain with it and am afraid to move. Carefully, he feels around and then slips out, stripping his gloves. I'm embarrassed, pissed, and hurt, and feel tears prick at the violation.

The doctor puts my knees together and asks again when my last period was and if I'm on birth control. "I'm giving you a birth control shot regardless of your answer, so you may as well tell me. Some medications don't mix, and you don't want to be ill here. There is no option of an ER visit." That fact alone scares me into answering.

"I'm already on the Depo, and I'm due in a week, I think. I'm not sure what time or day it is." He doesn't bother to answer, just swabs my arm and gives me the injection, before checking the silver watch on his wrist.

"Again, I am truly sorry. I don't believe you will fare well here, and I will be seeing you again. I have to go examine the others. Please get dressed, and I will have the guards escort you to get some food."

Won't fare well here? Is he fucking kidding me? And if others do fare well, what kind of people are they? How bad is this about to get?

I quickly get up from the table, not wanting to give the guards a chance to come in here while I'm mostly nude. Grabbing a few tissues, I clean myself up, noticing a pink tinge on the contrasting white. I freaking hate gynecological exams for this reason. Always so sensitive and then I'm sore for the rest of the day. Not to mention the ass stuck his finger in mine, and now that's not feeling so hot either. Not that I'm a prude, but Rex had never pushed it that far, and he was the majority of my good experiences with sex. I get dressed, cracking the door to let the guards know I'm ready and step out in between them, following the first one down the hall with the other bringing up the rear.

Rex

I knew I was going to be asked questions and get an exam. Emmett and I were both briefed on what would be done, but damn, the doc *really* had to go there. I'm not amused by my squishy ass or the hard on I got from that bastard thoroughly checking my prostate. Not to mention the questions that were asked, about myself— and Lark too. I can only imagine what Lark went through, as it was a good forty-five minutes of waiting before the doc came in. When I asked the doctor about Lark, he said she was fine and done. I wanted to punch the man for touching her, even in a medical capacity. I also couldn't help but be amused that she'd given him shit. I just hoped her smart mouth hadn't gotten her into trouble.

I have to figure out a way to keep us all together because I don't think I can keep my cool and not blow our cover if she gets passed around, and that would end in us all being killed. I tip my head in my hands and listen to the others in the curtained off exam areas, answering their questions and receiving their inspections. This doctor was specifically brought in by Apollo just for Emmett and me. Now he gets two more patients to care for. Some of the answers I'm hearing make me raise my brows— Emmett is a bit of a freak; I figured Braeden would be, but *damn* on my partner. Guess he's more than qualified for this assignment. On the one hand, I'm glad Lark got a private room and wasn't being subjected to this, but on the other, I'm worried about where she is right now. As the doc finishes up with the others, I get dressed and wait to find out what's happening next.

Rex

I KNEW I was going to be asked questions and get an exam. Emmett and I were both briefed on what would be done, but damn, the doc *really* had to go there. I'm not amused by my squishy ass or the hard on I got from that bastard thoroughly checking my prostate. Not to mention the questions that were asked, about myself— and Lark too. I can only imagine what Lark went through, as it was a good forty-five minutes of waiting before the doc came in. When I asked the doctor about Lark, he said she was fine and done. I wanted to punch the man for touching her, even in a medical capacity. I also couldn't help but be amused that she'd given him shit. I just hoped her smart mouth hadn't gotten her into trouble.

I have to figure out a way to keep us all together because I don't think I can keep my cool and not blow our cover if she gets passed around, and that would end in us all being killed. I tip my head in my hands and listen to the others in the curtained off exam areas, answering their questions and receiving their inspections. This doctor was specifically brought in by Apollo just for Emmett and me. Now he gets two more patients to care for. Some of the answers I'm hearing make me raise my brows— Emmett is a bit of a freak; I figured Braeden would be, but *damn* on my partner. Guess he's more than qualified for this assignment. On the one hand, I'm glad Lark got a private room and wasn't being subjected to this, but on the other, I'm worried about where she is right now. As the doc finishes up with the others, I get dressed and wait to find out what's happening next.

4

DICTATOR MARCUS

Lark

I'm led into a mess hall of sorts; one end is a cafeteria and the other a shopping/laundry area. The first guard explains that the little free time we will receive will be in here to eat, get toiletries, or to do laundry. We're expected to clean up after ourselves, and this is considered a freedom that's earned. Any infractions will result in confinement and punishment. I can imagine how that will go, but is it really any different than what's already happening?

I try to surreptitiously look for exits, but the rear guard must have noticed that I'm casing the area. He rudely informs me that we're in the basement level, and even in the case of an emergency we aren't getting out of here— there are no exits. The guarded staircases and elevator bank are the only way out of here. I deflate a little at this. *I want Rex. No, that asshole can go screw himself. I want Braeden.*

As if thinking of Braeden has summoned him, he's brought in with Rex and Emmett. I go to run and embrace him, but both of my upper arms are grabbed. "No touching." *What a dick.*

I'm already tired of being manhandled, and it's only going to get worse from here. I see Rex slightly shake his head and ignore him, but when Braeden does it, I comply, earning me a glare from Rex.

Fuck you, Rex.

My eyes must express this well enough because his face goes to stony impassiveness. He's lost my respect, but I'll follow my bestie to Hell and back if needed.

Our little group is led to a line to get trays of food. After we're through collecting our lunch, or maybe dinner? I can't really tell what time it is from the fluorescent lighting, and there aren't any handy clocks hanging out either, but it's not breakfast food being served.

Regardless of what the guards said, I keep an eye out for any hint of an exit as we're led out to the hall and down a few door-ways. The guard in front opens the room into a type of sterile sitting/dining area like you would see in a halfway house. *Well, isn't that apt? If I stay here too long, I'll need to be admitted to one. May as well get used to it now.*

The room has utilitarian furniture in a kitchen and common area combo. A sectional sofa and a recliner with a coffee table and television in front of it take up a portion of the room. The dining table is like the one my old school lunch-room had, with bench seating, except adult-sized. On the far side of the room a fridge, and kitchenette are set up— complete with a wall-mounted oven.

Rex and Emmett take seats on one side together, while I move around the table to sit opposite them. *No way am I sitting next to that cunt muffin right now.*

Braeden, letting out a gusty sigh, sits next to me, opening his mouth as if to say something, until I shoot him a glare that shuts him up quick.

The lead guard addresses us. "Leave your trays on the counter over there, someone will be by to pick them up later.

The bathroom and bedroom are through that door, go through the bedroom to get to the bathroom. Towels, extra clothing, and toiletries have been stocked in the hall closet."

Oh, goody, the kidnappers will let us bathe and sleep. They're so awesome! I snort at my thoughts, earning a glare from the guard. *Oops.*

He continues, "There will be guards posted in the halls, and there are security cameras. Don't try anything, or there will be consequences." The guard looks at me as he says this. I can't tell if he thinks I'll try something, or if I'm the one being held over the guys' heads— probably both. With his little speech over, they all leave. We finish our food in silence and put our trays on the counter as instructed.

"I'm going for a shower, I feel disgusting." Not waiting for a response, I leave the table. Frankly, I couldn't care less what they think.

I get a towel and shower supplies from the hall closet and find the list of rules on the door— ignoring them completely after seeing one of them says to shave daily. *Whatever. They can kiss my ass on that one.* Looking around, I see folded clothing on some of the shelves, and after some searching, find a tank top and some yoga pants that are my size, along with panties, but no bra. I sigh and decide to wash mine out and put it back on later— I'm just going to bed after I get done with my shower anyway.

I notice there's another door at the end of the short hall, with a keypad next to the doorframe, and when I try it, it's locked. Not really sure I want to know what's kept in there anyway, I turn to the only other door and open it. Inside, it's set up like a large dorm room. Four beds with nightstands and lamps— nothing else— not even windows. Although, I suppose windows wouldn't be down this far in the ground. That thought gives me the shivers, what if there were an emergency? Or the structure above us collapses?

Shaking off my morbidness, I continue through the open door, noting a decent-sized tub and shower combo, counter, a sink with a few drawers under it, and a toilet; still very utilitarian. I set my items out and start the water. *I hope they have a good supply of hot water, I want a shower, then a good soak.* Stripping down, I climb in, washing my hair and body before rinsing, so I can engage the tub stopper, letting it fill enough until I can lower myself in. I must doze off a bit in the hot water because I wake up to the sound of a knock on the door.

"Lark? You alright in there?" Braeden, he must have been worried. I've been in here long enough to prune, so I guess he probably thought I drowned myself. *Eh, I'll reserve that option if needed.*

"I'm fine, be right out." I push off my maudlin thoughts and pull the stopper to drain the water. I get out, drying myself off and dressing. I'm still brushing my hair as I open the door to find Braeden is standing there with concern plastered on his face.

"Do I need to worry about you checking out on me?" He flinches as he asks this, and for him to bring it up means he's really, extremely worried about me. His mom killed herself when he was a teenager, and he's the one who found her— slit her wrists in the tub.

I hug him, dirty clothes, body odor, and all. Not that he really smells that bad, Braeden always smells like home. "Of course not, I would never do that to you. If things get that bad, I'll talk to you about it. We'll get out of here, it can't be that long before Rex can get a message out and get us free. Really, I don't care about their stupid assignment at this place, we didn't sign up for this crap. I'll play along as well as I can until we're rescued." Reassuring us both the best I can, I let him go and step back, feeling guilty for even thinking about it.

"Ditto, Birdie." He uses the comforting nickname he gave me the day we met.

"I'm gonna go get into one of those beds, make sure you're between me and Rex. I'm liable to smother him with a pillow in his sleep if he gets too close to me. Who knows what that man was thinking, cheating would have been preferable to *this*." Making my way back into the bedroom I choose the bed closest to the bathroom and finish brushing my hair before climbing into the bed between the stiff, industrial sheets, that smell strongly of bleach. I'm almost asleep before my head hits the pillow.

5

NOT FOLLOWING THE RULES

I wake up to low voices and the sound of the shower running, not moving or opening my eyes yet, but I can hear Braeden and Emmett talking.

"How long do you think before we can get out of here?" Braeden asks.

"Let's not discuss that openly, never know who might be listening in, and I like my head attached to my body. I'll let you know as soon as I know anything. I'm more worried right now, over what's going to be done with the two of you. You weren't originally part of the buyer's acquisition. I don't know how Apollo plans to keep you from the general rotation."

That same concern has been running in the back of my mind since I woke up and found out what had happened, and it seems Braeden shares my thoughts.

Braeden continues to voice his concerns, "I'm worried about Lark, women tend to get it worse in these types of situations. Frankly, I'm used to getting buttfucked, fucking others, and sucking dick. It's not like I'm a straight guy getting his anal cherry popped. Can't say being forced into it is going to be a cakewalk, but I have less orifices than Lark."

Oh, shit. I'm gonna get fucked in the ass. Rex and I played a bit with that, but only in little ways, and a finger rubbing on the outside is a lot different than a dick on the inside. *At least Rex is going to get the same treatment.* It would be kinda hot to see him getting mounted. I've had my finger in his ass during blow jobs, and he seemed to like it well enough, but in our case, what was good for the gander was not happening with the goose. I snicker silently. That makes me feel a little better, but also a tad ashamed for feeling it at the same time.

"Not much we can do on that right now." Emmett answers him. "We'll just have to try our best to keep her with us exclusively."

Oh my god, I'm going to have to fuck my best friend and *Rex's partner, and they'll all be watching and fucking each other as well.* I'm going to have a fucking panic attack. I want to go home. I curse Rex again as I stretch and sit up, causing the guys to stop talking.

"How long was I asleep for?"

Braeden answers me. "A couple hours, how are you feeling?"

"A little better, still woke up here though." I grimace at that fact.

The water in the bathroom shuts off, and a few minutes later, Rex comes out in sweats, barefoot, and rubbing a towel over his wet hair. Asshole needs to put a shirt on. I turn away, refusing to look at him.

He stops in front of me, but I still won't look up at him. "Are you going to be angry with me forever? I tried to do the right thing, Lark. I never meant to drag you into this." I glance up long enough to glare into his sapphire eyes, and yes, I really *do* still want to blacken them.

"Fuck you, Rex. Get me out of here," I say, my voice monotone. I need to distance myself from this, from him.

Braeden comes over to my bed and pulls me into his lap,

wrapping his arms around my torso, making me feel safe for the moment, but I know it won't last. Rex looks on disapprovingly, but I don't care. He can go fuck himself.

Emmett speaks to me instead, probably hoping I'm less angry at him. "Lark, you're going to have to be prepared to not get out of here right away. I'm not sure how long it will take for a message to get to our contact, and then for an extraction team to be sent in. All we can do is stay alive until they get here. I know we've never really bonded much, but I wouldn't wish this on anyone. I came of my own free will, as did Rex. I'll do my best to respect you."

I'm kind of surprised he would make such a declaration. He hasn't come around the house much when I've been there, even though he lives there. I think Rex asked him to make himself scarce after he walked in on us naked, me going down on Rex as he sat on the couch. He'd stood in the doorway and stared a little too long, even if it was an accident. I guess he's probably about to get his curiosity satisfied.

Realizing I should probably say something, I respond, "Thank you, Emmett. I appreciate it." I stay snuggled for a bit in Brade's lap until the sound of the main door opening and closing interrupts us. I tense, and Braeden holds me tighter, as Rex and Emmett stand to block us both. Apollo and his little buddy, Marcus, appear in the doorway. Marcus, the one in front, addresses us.

"All of you use the toilet, then clean your genitals thoroughly with these, put them in the trash, not the toilet, when you're through. Once you've finished, come into the room at the end of the hall, the last person in must close the door and make sure it latches." Marcus throws each of us a pack of wipes, and Rex catches them, turning without a word, and walks to the bathroom doorway, leaning against the frame.

"What the fuck?" This from Emmett. "Right down to it then,

huh? 'Sanitizing wipes for the perineal area'." He reads off the packet he received. "Lovely. Who's first, then?"

"You and I will go first, then Lark, and Braeden can bring up the rear. I don't want her in first or last on anything. If we can keep her in the middle, we can at least try to protect her." Rex pushes off the doorjamb to go into the bathroom, coming out a few minutes later with no expression on his face as he heads out the door.

Emmett does the same, then it's my turn, and Braeden kisses my forehead before ushering me off his lap and toward the bathroom. A deep flush creeps up my chest, turning my face red, knowing that everyone knows what I'm doing, and from the fact that I know they had to do it too.

My hands are shaking as I close the door and read the instructions. Just like when you need to pee in a cup at the doctor's office. I do my business, wipe correctly with three wipes, wash my hands, and leave the bathroom, unable to look at my best friend as I pass.

The door with the electronic lock is standing open, but I can't see directly into the room thanks to the little entry area blocking the view. There's enough space in it for two people, and I can see it turns at least two corners before it ends. I think its purpose is to actually keep either room from seeing into the other, even with the door open. I linger at the second corner, getting my courage up. The timeout allows Braeden to catch up with me, and I reach back for his hand. With a deep breath, I round the corner, and just stare with my mouth hanging open.

It's a fucking sex fiend's deviant playground. There are odd things all over, not to mention the clear cupboards and drawers filled with objects. All the surfaces and fronts of the counters and cupboards appear to be plexiglass, not quite as crystal clear as regular glass. Guess it would hold up better in this type of area. Honestly, I'm not even sure where to begin. Completely petrified, I'm squeezing the shit out of Brade's hand, and have zero interest in letting go.

The room is large, nearly twice the size of the apartment we just left. There are several chair type things that look like a cross between a dentist's chair and a gynecological exam table, but with more arms and a little slimmer. A shiver runs across my skin looking at them. There are two sling/swing contraptions hung next to each other on sliding tracts and stocks set up near those. On the wall is what I think is called a St. Andrew's Cross, although I doubt saintly things are performed with it. *Who knows, maybe that one was the saint of perverts?* On another wall are bars extending out like in a handicapped toilet and metal holes inset in the wall between them. Not sure I want to find out what exactly those are for either. The cabinets are full of sex toys and gadgets and other equipment I can't quite make out from where I stand. There are stainless steel rolling tables set next to the different stations, the type you find in medical facilities.

I don't want to step into the room, but Braeden takes the lead and pulls me with him to stand near the others. Apollo is sitting in a chair near a counter, and Marcus is doing something around the side of it, leaving Apollo to address us this time.

"I've managed to add the two new ones to the program." His wording is odd, like we aren't people. It gives me the creeps. "Same conditions apply as for the originals, with the exception that if the buyer doesn't want all four of you, the other two," he gestures, indicating me and Braeden, "will be auctioned off at the end of the training program. That gives us six weeks to complete this. Note, however, that any insubordination will be punished. I cannot avoid that, so please consider your actions carefully. You never know when you are being watched, and I cannot keep the jammers I have in place on indefinitely without arousing suspicion. Marcus will take over while I observe."

I can't decide if I should throw my hissy now or bide my time. I don't want to just willingly take this, but I'm not sure what other option I have. The guys seem to be going along with it, and I can't rebel without their support unless it's more serious than it has been so far. I decide just to go along for now, pick my battles, or whatever shit applies to this situation.

That thought lasts all of sixty seconds before I balk. Marcus takes the stage and begins speaking, well, dictating is more like it. "You will all strip, then fold and place your clothing in these bins. I am going to number you instead of using your names. You," he points at Rex, "are One." Points next at Emmett, then Braeden, and finally at me, numbering us as he goes. " You are Two, you will be Three, and you are Four. You will learn to respond to them or be punished." He sets out the bins on the counter.

The men move to do as instructed, but I stand there and cross my arms defiantly. No way am I getting naked in front of five guys. I only know three, and only two have seen me completely naked and only one on purpose. Marcus looks at me, and I stare back. "You will do as you were instructed, Four, or I will remove them myself, and you will not receive any type of covering back for the rest of the day. Am I clear?" The frostiness coming off his tone is enough to have the guys moving back toward me protectively. I can't have them getting hurt over my modesty. I sigh and wave them off as I move past them. Reaching the counter, I take my clothes off, placing them in the bin after folding them.

Marcus is staring again. "You didn't shave. Did you not see the instructions in the closet?" I'm trying not to gape at the naked men around me. They're all buff and hot, even my bestie. And hairless. *Where the hell did Rex and Brade's chest hair go? Did they shave their armpits?* I'm so distracted trying not to get caught ogling, that it takes a moment to process what Marcus was saying. *Oh yeah. Should have known I would get in trouble for that one.* I nod my head, not wanting to open my mouth, and get myself into more trouble. It's then that I notice that all the men are bare downstairs. *They look like little baby birds, bald.* I almost giggle out loud. *Yep, legs are hairless too. What the hell?*

"Yes, you saw the notice? Then you deliberately defied the rules. And what is it that you find so amusing?" I school my expression and shake my head. No way am I saying what I just thought. "I'll set up waxing for you when we are finished here, then, since shaving seems to be too tedious for you. And, for your insubordination, the men will get full waxes as well." *Ah, shit. I hate waxing. Brade is gonna kick my ass.* I still say nothing, and Marcus continues on after a parting glare directed my way. He gets one right back. Rex and Braeden both sigh audibly. *Huh, guess they can find middle ground if it involves being annoyed at me.*

6
CRASH COURSE

"Gentlemen, I've read over your answers on your sexual experience. I have tailored plans to each of you. Four, get in this chair over here." I docilely go over to the chair he specifies, a vinyl piece with some type of soft fabric attached instead of the usual paper runner a normal exam table would have. I climb on as the guys watch. I stiffly allow Marcus to manipulate my limbs. My arms are taken out slightly and secured. A band goes under my breasts across my chest until it's snug, while my feet are placed in stirrups with supporting leather straps behind my knees that are somehow attached underneath me. The feet are drawn up and out to be slightly above and next to my hips. It's putting a bit of a strain on them, but nothing terrible. My eyes close in embarrassment until a ratcheting sound starts, and they fly open at the sound. The straps tighten on my knees and pull them outward until I wince with the strain. One click back and I relax a little until a portion of table drops out from under my ass leaving me feeling the cool air and five gazes on my nether regions. I don't have much time to process this before the top flips down and my head tips back making my mouth parallel to my neck. *This*

can't be a good thing. Marcus leaves me like that, much to my furious embarrassment, and turns to the staring men. The baby birds are not improved upon from this angle. *Hey, they were staring already, so that makes them fair game in my book.*

"Line up over here, lean over the pommel, and reach for the grips on the other side." At his direction, I see that I missed a contraption. From my position, I can see exactly what's going on, and while the guys' backs are to me, they can't see that I'm watching.

I feel eyes on me, and I turn to find Apollo is watching me observe them. The fucker winks at me. That's when I notice he has a slim tube in his hand, and he's coming toward me with it. "Just a small amount of lubricant for prep." I hold my tongue at his explanation even when he presses it into my vagina and depresses the plunger. Ignoring the weirdo once he's finished, I turn my attention back to what's happening across from me.

There is a shorter adjustable pommel horse, like you see in gymnastics, with two handles in front of it. Rex is up first, and he leans over it, but apparently, it's too tall for what Marcus wants, so he lowers it with hydraulics and extends the handles. This causes Rex to bend over further and squat down until I can see his asshole and balls hanging between his legs. Marcus taps the inside of his feet, and Rex spreads them further, giving me a better view and, presumably, Marcus better access.

"Soon, you'll be doing this for each other. For the first few sessions I will do it." He wheels over a tray filled with different-sized silicone butt plugs, a pump bottle of lube, and a box of what look like finger-sized condoms. *Must have been what he was working on at the counter.* I notice he slips the finger condoms on his first two fingers and thumb. Now knowing what the pommel is for, anticipation builds as I watch the proceedings. I can't deny I'm getting turned on already, which is probably the point, despite my trepidation. Marcus pumps some lube between his fingers and rubs it between them. He slicks his thumb around Rex's anus, and Rex flinches his cheeks together.

"Keep them spread!"

With that, he kicks Rex's feet further apart, making him squat down deeper and effectively keeping him spread open. *Oh, god. I can feel my own ass tingling in anticipation.* Marcus sits on a rolling stool and places his thumb back on Rex's hole, slowly rubbing in circles, probing just a little. Suddenly, as if he's run out of patience, he switches it up and slides his forefinger in to the first knuckle working it around. Slowly, it disappears to the second and hits the base of the third knuckle. He pushes in and out a few times then begins hooking it to come in and out in a twisting motion that makes Rex groan. *Fuck, my cunt is throbbing, who knew I would enjoy watching so much?* Marcus withdraws and then presses forward with both middle and forefinger together causing Rex to groan again, but I'm not sure if it's in pleasure or pain. He repeats the same motions as before except this time when he's done, he tilts his arm for more leverage and really digs forward. Rex gasps, and now it's a pleasurable moan; I recognize it. Noticing he's getting hard, I realize Marcus must be manipulating his prostate.

Rex is panting by the time Marcus removes his fingers. He selects a plug about the length of his fingers but a little thicker than the two of them together at the base. He coats it liberally in lube and breaches Rex's ass with one hand braced on his lower back. As it slides up and reaches its widest point, Rex grunts, and his balls draw up. With what looks like a pop, his muscle gives. The plug sinks home and settles in, the flange-like rim keeping it in place. There's a small ring attached to the end, and Marcus gives it a couple quick tugs to check its snugness, I'm guessing, garnering a flinch from Rex. He must be satisfied with it as he pats him on the ass and turns to Emmett as though saying, "You're next."

I might enjoy this one on purpose. *Sketchy angel boy is smokin' in the raw, all gilded ivory and angles. Down, girl* Rex gingerly stands up and avoids meeting my eyes when he notices me watching. Instead, he awkwardly walks to stand next to Braeden. I feel a little sorry for him now since I think he's bitten off more than he'd anticipated with this assignment. *Maybe you shouldn't have lied to your girlfriend about being a reporter.*

I start paying attention again as Emmett assumes the position and gets the pommel horse adjusted for him as well. Marcus immediately starts him out in the deeper squat, and this time he goes for a glove. I'm nervous for him, and I don't even like him that much. I see he's already half hard, must be from watching Rex. That *was* kind of hot. Marcus doesn't bother with the thumb, going straight for the first finger routine, then the second with barely any time in between. He digs those fingers down into Emmett and does the same thing as he did to Rex, getting a moan and an instant woody in return. On his way to exiting Emmett's ass, Marcus scissors his fingers out to the sides in a vee motion causing Emmett to groan.

The plug Marcus selects this time is at least half the size and width of the one Rex received, and its tip is more blunt and wide. Marcus lubes it up and starts pressing inward, and Emmett starts rapidly breathing immediately. Marcus continues to push until Emmett's hole is spread wide before it contracts after the widest point disappears, letting the plug settle in. He gets the ass pat and stands up, taking his place next to Rex. He doesn't make eye contact with anyone either.

I can actually feel my outer lips getting slick, and the fact that I'm turned on initiates a wave of shame to course through me. It's hard to hold on to the feeling though, and I let it go.

Marcus leaves Emmett to approach Braeden, and I'm not really sure how I feel about watching. I'm curious, but I also feel like a bit of a perv. I know he likes guys, that's never been a secret. It also makes me wonder if Marcus or Apollo are getting turned on by this too. My wandering thoughts are brought back to the current events as Braeden is quickly in position, and Marcus has a new glove on. Guess my ex-boyfriend is the anal virgin here, well, besides the little bit I'd done with him.

Marcus dips in one lubed finger, then two, and finally three into his hole. Braeden stiffens at the third, eventually relaxing after some stretching. His cock twitches as soon as Marcus starts that digging, and I think he may be getting off from it by the movement of his hips.

Did I mention that my best friend is hung? I've only seen dicks that big in porn and maybe not even there. Though I haven't watched much either, so there's that to consider. My attention returns to Braeden as Marcus pulls back until the tip of his thumb can meet up with the other three fingers and slides back in. Braeden finally grunts and continues to do so as Marcus bends his thumb and pops it in and out going in a circle. When he's done, he gets a very large plug out. I wince in sympathy.

It appears to be about five inches long and shaped like an oversized egg. The indent at the bottom, that the tight ring of muscle grips, is almost as wide. Marcus starts with the blunt tip, and I can see that Braeden is breathing deep and trying to relax his ass. His pucker is breached and begins to expand, continuing to do so until Marcus reaches to spread his cheeks further with his other hand. He pushes with a twisting motion and then stops at the widest portion. I want to protest the treatment, but Braeden lets out a long low sound before his ring relaxes, and the plug slides home.

He rests for a moment, and I don't blame him. When he stands and sees me watching, his cheeks darken, and he looks ashamed. I try to smile at him to let him know he shouldn't be. It wasn't his choice, and I shouldn't have watched. I'll have to discuss how we want to handle this later because I don't want it damaging our friendship.

∾

MARCUS, ever the dictator, gestures the guys over to me. Now, I'm really nervous, and I can feel my own fluids running down my ass crack announcing to everyone just how turned on the scene has gotten me. It's my turn to blush in shame. Although, I shouldn't be worried, as these guys are about to be balls deep in me. Apollo has been quiet the entire time, and I'm afraid to look and see what he's been up to now that I remember he's in the room. *Ostrich, I'll be an ostrich. Safer that way.*

"Three, I want you up here at her head. One, on your knees, in front of her pussy, Two, you'll be assisting me and getting your next size." *Looks like Emmett's gonna get stretched today.* That can't be good for me. "Four, since you declined to answer most of the questions from Dr. Martins, we will be doing a rigorous crash course." The dick, I think he's enjoying this for sure now. "Two, bring me the tray. These are pre-loaded syringes of lube. They're thin, so they don't hold much, and you'll need to apply multiple applications." *Fucker, you're gonna regret this.* "Three, put your dick in her mouth and start pumping, don't go past her throat yet."

Oh, god, I'm going to have my best friend's dick in my mouth. I meet his eyes and nod my permission. He looks excited and miserable at the same time if that's possible. It's an odd combination, anyway. I stick out my tongue to wet his dick with it before he slides in, almost hitting my throat right away before backing up. I almost laugh at how many 'just the tip' jokes I could make since, with his length, that's all that is fitting in my mouth. Laughing with his cock in my mouth might be bad though. I'll save the jokes for later— if there's a later to be had out of this place.

He continues moving in and out shallowly, with my mouth stretched wide around his girth, in a slow languorous pace while I suck on him. I focus on not getting him with my teeth until my attention, and from what I can tell, his too, is drawn to what's happening below my waist. I feel a squirt of cold on my ass then an intrusion that leaks more coldness as it pushes in. It withdraws, only to happen several more times.

Under Marcus' instruction, my anus is probed by a thin flexible tube with a harder bulbous tip, and what feels like some kind of rod inside the tube. Once it reaches past a depth of several inches, I begin to worry. When it hits the uncomfortable zone, I tense, then it hurts sharply, eliciting a squeal from me around Braeden's dick. At that point, it stops but doesn't retreat. I'm still trying to suck while waiting to see what happens next when I feel a pressure inside my ass and what sounds like the bulb of a blood pressure cuff being pumped up.

Rex, bless his informative heart, protests, "She's never had anything in her ass. You're hurting her." *Kill me now, could this be any more embarrassing?* Braeden grunts in surprise. *Yes, yes it could.*

"She should have thought about that before refusing to answer." Dickface Marcus continues his narrative. "This is an inflatable trainer. It only goes up to a small size, but it will get you used to it and allow for a larger sized inflatable next time. Two, pump it until you can see it spread her about a half inch in diameter from the outside." I'd kick Emmett if I had a free leg. Probably why they're restrained, I muse. *Why the hell can't I concentrate?* "One, get to work with your mouth, then work up to three fingers in her pussy. Three, you have six strokes to get balls deep." *Um, what? That thing ain't gonna fit. I'm gonna puke.*

With Marcus' directives complete, my ass inflates, Rex starts licking my clit and slides a finger in me, while Braeden takes my head in both hands. "Breathe shallowly, and swallow when you want to gag." Brade whispers to me.

I'd glare at him, but since my view is currently of his taint, it wouldn't have much impact. At least his dick sucking advice is coming from experience. I get the breathing part down, but as soon as he hits the back of my throat and holds there, I gag involuntarily. It results in my ass and pussy flexing around the intrusions in them, sending shockwaves through me.

On the second attempt, I swallow, and he makes it halfway in before my throat closes, refusing to take more. My jaw hurts from being opened so wide, and I don't know if I can get this fucking anaconda down my throat. On the fifth try, he's holding and still pressing forward, coaching me to relax as he pushes my head back further. A quick slide forward, and he's in, and now I can't breathe at all. I panic, gurgling a noise out. He instantly pulls out, trailing saliva, and Marcus appears with a basin right on time for me to heave up phlegm into. My mortification is complete.

"Deflate the tubing, remove it, and put it in the wash bin." *Oh, God. Wash bin? Aren't you supposed to prep for anal?* Every time I think it can't get worse, it does. I figure I have a fifty-fifty chance of things being kosher down there since the amount of lube that has been put in could double as an enema, and I'm not feeling any bathroom urges. I decide I don't want to know, after all they're in the same predicament.

"Three, pick up the pace but don't orgasm. Two, when you're done with that tubing, come over here." As the tubing is removed, my body relaxes in relief. Rex is still going to town on my box and has the three requested fingers working magic. He's always been good at this. *God, I'm getting close.* "Two, place these on her nipples." I can't see, but nothing good has ever come of putting objects on nipples, in my opinion. I feel Emmett hold one breast, gathering my nipple in his long fingers, then a pinch that rapidly intensifies. I yell, but with Braeden going in and out of my throat, it's muffled and makes him moan and pause his movement. *Down my throat.*

I can't breathe, and I involuntarily bite down a bit on reflex.

"Fuck, sorry little bird." I'd say sorry too, except for, ya know, the dick plugging my mouth.

At the same time, Emmett grabs my other nipple and repeats the torture. This time my yell can be heard as Braeden is quick enough to remove his appendage from the reach of my teeth.

My bestie ain't stupid.

Rex pauses, and I sense and feel that he's looking up. He resumes his licking with more gusto than before. What he's witnessing must be turning him on, or he's in competition with Braeden.

Probably a little of both.

Meanwhile, Marcus is still bossing Emmett around. "Two, hook this together and use it on her clit when I tell you." *Hook what, and put it where, now? Dammit, I can't see!* The sadistic maestro just doesn't quit, and my nipples are already on fire. Braeden resumes getting his blowjob, Rex is still busy on my downstairs, so it's apparent when I feel him move a little to the side and withdraw his fingers. "Relax your ass, this is bigger," is all the warning I get.

I hum in protest as I feel a slicked up, blunt tipped plug pushing in. It hurts as it pops through the opening of my ass. Marcus pauses a moment, then continues pushing in. *What the fuck is he using?* I'm groaning and trying, futilely, to escape as it gets deeper and wider. When I scream with a dick down my throat again, Marcus tells Rex to suck hard. Rex's lips and tongue isolate my clit with fingers to either side, spreading the skin to make it taut and that much more sensitive. My anus flexes at the pleasure, and I moan around Braeden's dick as the plug is literally sucked into my ass with rhythmic internal pulses. The sensation is so intense, and the plug is so wide, that I can't decide if it hurts that bad or not.

When it settles, Rex moves back into position, then he pauses and holds very still with his fingers still in my pussy. I feel those fingers tense as he groans. *I guess he just got an upgrade on his plug, too.* He resumes with mouth and hand, and now Marcus is telling Braeden to pause for three counts at the full depth of each penetration. With him doing that, it gets even harder to breathe properly. Rex is working me over, bumping the plug repeatedly, and I'm in sensory overload with burning nipples. When I start to come, Marcus tells Braeden to hold, and I can't breathe at all. My whole body draws up, fighting the restraints that refuse to give. Marcus threatens to do it himself if Braeden, who must have protested, moves.

"Two, pull back her hood and clamp now." I'm so out of it from the lack of oxygen that it doesn't register what is happening at first. Until I feel my engorged clit exposed and a clamp tightened over it.

Rex's fingers are still going to town, and someone is twisting the plug in my backside. I'm clamping down on everything, my muscles seizing, as I feel lightheaded enough to see black spots, and the clamp on my clit begins to pulse with shocks. The nipple clamps are released, causing me to screech as the blood rushes back into them, and as I'm in the middle of the strongest orgasm of my life someone pulls the plug out of my tightened ass, compounding the intensity and length of the orgasm.

The last thing I hear is Rex cursing about strangled fingers, and Braeden's shout as I pass out.

7

YOU'RE PUTTING THAT WHERE?

Braeden

"Shit!" Lark passed out, and the way her throat convulsed around my cock every time she choked, made me start to come. I'm so worked up from the deep throating and watching the scene play out that I wasn't paying attention. Gripping the base of my dick, I withdraw quickly so I don't drown her with my semen. I'm horrified at the dark thrill I got— the sensation her constricting throat evoked as she struggled for air flat did it for me— shame fills me, even though I was made to do it.

Unfortunately, it's too late not to come and as soon as I'm clear of her mouth my tip is aimed right at Rex, shooting my load straight into his face. *Oh, fuck. I just jizzed right in my best friend's boyfriend's mouth.* It's *so* not my fault that he was yelling about Lark clamping on his fingers and his mouth happened to be open. Rex and Emmett both look at me in shock. "I'm sorry. I tried to stop it. I was afraid she would choke when she passed out." I stumble out my apology.

Rex wipes his tongue on his arm, glaring at me, while

Emmett hands him a couple wipes to help clean up. Apollo is in his chair, laughing his ass off, with Marcus smirking as if he'd planned all of this. *No one is* that *good.* He goes on with his instructions, unconcerned about Lark.

"Three, go get in the chair right there." Marcus is indicating the one next to Lark. He's gone around to her head and is lifting the support back into place. Rex is cleaning her up now too. I'm glad he's at least taking care of her. "One, get in the chair next to three." Emmett is just standing there with a hard dick and a plug in his ass, watching. I guess we all have full asses now that I think about it. It makes walking uncomfortable for sure. I gingerly ease into the chair, avoiding pressure on my backside by leaning back. Rex does the same, although he's pussyfooting a lot more than I am. Not that I blame him if he's never had anything in his backdoor.

Marcus secures us both and positions us the same as Lark, but with our heads and torsos slightly elevated. Guess we won't be sucking dick— yet. Our positions are indicative that we're supposed to watch what happens. I can see the end of the little black plug poking out of Rex. It's hard to take my gaze from it, but then Marcus steps between my legs with a glove on again. He grips the ring at the bottom and starts working the plug out. It's almost as bad as it was going in now that it's had time to get dry in there. The lube was silicone-based at least. When it finally pops free, I sigh in relief only to groan when he immediately enters me with three fingers full of lube, generously rubbing it around. He withdraws, handing Emmett a condom and indicating the lube. So that's the next step, getting fucked. My dick twitches a little in anticipation. I've always thought Emmett was hot, but I never knew he might swing that way. His dark angel looks just do it for me, and I'll take whatever perks are to be found in the situation. Marcus moves away as Emmett lines his dick up with my hole.

Lark

I come back to consciousness slowly and open my eyes to see Apollo sitting in a new spot. One where he has a full-on view of all my lady bits. I'm not sure how I feel about that when I notice his attention is not on me, but on the scenes next to me.

Marcus and Rex are both watching as Emmett lines his condom-covered dick up with my best friend's ass. Emmett makes contact and widens his stance before pressing forward. He's actually about the same size as Rex, long and not too wide. As he spreads his legs, I notice the plug is still in him; it flexes with every movement. I can't imagine having to walk around with it in. He presses in, and there is little resistance from all the lube I see shining on them both under the industrial lighting. He pauses a little ways in, and when Braeden relaxes, he thrusts in until their pelvises meet. Braeden lets out a moan with his face pinched. I can't tell if he likes it or not. Emmett pulls all the way out, and I see Braeden gaping open as his anus slowly starts to close. Before it's completely closed again, Emmett plunges back in. He continues for several minutes until I see Braeden getting hard again, at which point Emmett changes it up and keeps up a steady, bruising pace. His face is a mask of concentration, and his beautiful muscles are well-defined by the hard flex he's maintaining. I'm surprised to feel myself getting worked up again from watching.

Movement brings my attention over to Rex and Marcus. Marcus is removing his plug, using a long syringe to apply lube on his stretched rim, then sinking it deeply after the toy comes out, to administer it inside. He repeats the process of lubrication twice more until it's dripping out of Rex. *That's a lot of lube.*

Marcus grabs something and goes over to the other couple,

making them pause. They're both slightly trembling. Marcus takes a leather ring with a strap and buckle around it. He fits the ring over Braeden's cock then slips it over his balls as well. Threading the end around, he tightens it and fastens it with the buckle. I know my eyes are as wide as Braeden's. He winces a little when his cock twitches with Emmett still in him. *What the hell is that? I've heard of cock rings, but this looks like nothing I've ever seen. Can he even come with that on?* Marcus pulls out a measuring tape, holding it up to Braeden's dick. Walking away, he indicates for Emmett to resume.

I watch with rapt curiosity as Marcus pulls out a drawer, reading the print on a package inside before opening it to reveal a black dildo. Appearing to be glass, it's definitely not flexible, and it's roughly the length of Braeden's dick, but not the width. Maybe about half of it. Rex looks nervous as Marcus moves in. Marcus doesn't hesitate when he gets to Rex; as he was walking, he'd coated the dildo in lube. *This place must spend a fortune on the stuff.* The glass is slightly pointed and breaks right into Rex's anus, spreading it wide without a hiccup. He keeps pushing up until Rex is straining the bonds holding him and making noises in the back of his throat. He stops there for a moment, then pushes in and out in short strokes, working it deeper each time. When it looks as if the last inch just isn't going to go in, Marcus reclines Rex's torso back some and changes the angle of his legs. Still holding the base of the dildo, I see him apply more pressure, the gritting of Rex's teeth becoming almost audible.

I can feel I'm wet again, and I can't take my eyes off Rex being penetrated so fully that it makes my own ass feel hollow. Not something I'd have thought to notice or experience before today. Slowly, it slides in the last bit, and Marcus just holds it there to let Rex acclimate before rotating it and rocking it back and forth without ever withdrawing it. Rex is still hard, so he can't be hating it too badly. Eventually, Marcus starts working it all the way out, then back in again, gradually picking up speed until he notices that Emmett is losing his rhythm. He abruptly pulls the dildo out, setting it aside and leaving Rex's stretched hole empty.

Rolling his stool over behind Emmett, he reaches between his legs to massage his balls, and at the same time he starts pulling the long plug out. With the sounds Emmett is making he's in the throes of one heck of an orgasm. He's buried to the hilt, hips pumping forward every other second, while his ass holds its grip on the plug until Marcus finally drags out of him. For a moment, he collapses partially over Braeden after it's over, catching his breath. Marcus is impatient, unstrapping Braeden before pulling Emmett upright and out of his behind. Letting Braeden up, Marcus doesn't bother to clean him up. Instead, Marcus leaves his asshole sloppy with all the lube. *Such a nice guy to let him clean up.* I wince in sympathy at the red, tender-looking skin between Brade's cheeks. Marcus tells Emmett to take the chair Braeden has just vacated. I wrinkle my nose at him not even bothering to clean the mess off before Emmett collapses on it.

Marcus unhooks the cock ring and rubs lube on Braeden's dick, which is standing at full attention. Going back over to Rex, he puts another tube of lubrication in him. *What the hell, is he planning to stick a foot in there? Is that a thing? I hope that's not a thing.*

"Three, you'll be fucking One, if that isn't obvious by now." *Not a foot, then. Phew, but with the bat my bestie is packing there's no such thing as too much lube.* I wonder if Marcus purposely did this because of the group dynamic?

Rex is vocal about his feelings, "You're going to, what? No way, he's *not* putting that in me— pick someone else." His mutiny is short-lived when Marcus flicks a sharp glance in my direction. "You've got to be kidding me, right now." He mutters, thumping his head back onto the headrest in defeat.

I'm gonna fuck him up for using me to control them. I'm fuming at the antics, and then of course my formerly level-headed best friend has to join in. Quietly, Braeden addresses Rex.

"I'm going to enjoy plowing your ass for what you've done to Lark." He says it with that smirk on his face, the one he gets when he's looking for trouble. He's considerate like that, it usually takes a lot to make him lose his cool. Unless you fuck with his family, i.e. me.

My bestie is the best, but I'm kinda worried he might do damage to Rex and regret it later. "Brade!" I hiss. They both glance over at me, as if they only now realize I'm awake. Sometimes, they're such idiots. Rex looks ashamed, and Braeden rolls his eyes but says nothing else.

"Get to it, boys." Marcus is barely paying attention, sorting through his drawers of torture tools again. Braeden moves up to Rex and starts dragging the head of his dick in small circles on Rex's asshole. I watch the scene in fascinated horror. Brade applies some pressure, and I see it slowly begin to widen. It doesn't go any further though, and it looks like someone trying to put on a beanie two sizes too small. He holds the head there and begins to work the end of his finger around the edges of the skin and muscle of Rex's lube-soaked entrance. Rex is groaning and gritting his teeth as Braeden's dick sinks in right past the mushroomed tip and he pauses for Rex to catch his breath. The taut skin blanches when he presses slightly further, causing Rex to make an odd noise. His dick has gone flaccid, so it's obvious to everyone that he is not enjoying this part, at least. Rocking back a tad, then pushing a bit forward, Braeden keeps trying to work his way in. With just a couple inches to go, Rex's flag is beginning to wave again. Braeden reaches up, grabbing Rex's shoulders, then curls his hips under and lunges up, breaching Rex completely and pulling a hoarse scream from his throat. Braeden mutters a sorry and holds very still. With Rex's cock half hard and deflating again, Braeden fills his palm with yet more lube to begin stroking Rex; using a twisting motion at the top before traveling back down to the base. Rex starts to relax, and Braeden begins to work in and out in long, slow strokes

I glance over, observing Apollo who is glued to the show. Emmett is half asleep, but the goings on have him at half-mast as well. Marcus turns his attention back to me and pulls out a skinny U-shaped metal rod with a handle. *Seriously, dude? I'm so done.* My limbs are aching, my throat is scratchy, and I can't decide what is more chafed; nether regions or nipples. I need something to drink, a shower, and the bathroom. Instead, Marcus is coming at me with this *thing.* One side is larger than the other and both have three balls on the ends graduating in size. Marcus greases them up, and I see the balls move inside the clear sleeve type thing housing them. Oddly enough the sizes change order when they're manipulated. On the upstroke, the largest end is at the top, on the way down it switches to last. As he gets closer, I realize it's not metal encased in clear silicone, but some kind of encapsulated gel bead clusters. I can't quite figure out the engineering behind the size changes. Maybe the pockets fill and escape through the channels depending on the pressure. I have a feeling I know who these are for. Apollo moves closer and leans in to sniff my crotch, to enjoy it as he inhales. My eyes go wide at the action.

"Would you mind?"

"Would I mind, what?" *WTF? How do I answer that after he scented me?*

"I wish to taste you." He's so proper and reserved in his speech. I doubt saying no would stop him. *Don't rock the crazy boat, birdbrain.* That's what Braeden would tell me— if he weren't boning my ex at the moment.

"Umm...okay I guess?" *Seriously, dude. What the fuck else am I gonna say? 'No, Mr. Scary-and-Nuttier-Than-Squirrel-Shit, you may not?' Righht— cuz that would go over well.* Trying to ignore him, I look over to the guys, and they're fully occupied. The little bit of attention Emmett's managing to muster up is also on those two. *Fucking, peachy.* I'm essentially alone with Marcus and Apollo while my best friend pounds Rex with skin-slapping noises. I don't understand why none of us are more concerned. I frown, thinking about it, but get sidetracked with the man between my spread and cramping legs.

Apollo leans over and gives me one long lick. From my opening to my clit, his tongue flat and firm. He lifts his head up, gazing at me, then leans in, holding eye contact, as he deliberately swirls his pointed tongue around my asshole. He takes his time, giving me a thorough rim job, before forcing his tongue in my back entrance. Fucking my ass with his tongue seems to be enjoyable for him as he keeps it up longer than I thought anyone would be interested in. He repeats the process on my pussy then sucks my clit like he'd suck on a nipple. He sits back with eyes dark and licks his lips. *Holy, fuck, that felt good. Also, I'd best not get a UTI from the swapsies.* I've never had a tongue in my ass. *Might have to take that up with a guy if I ever date again.* Marcus moves in on his stool, pushing a dazed Apollo out of the way. He'd *really* got off on eating my ass out. Marcus interrupts my thoughts again by pressing tubes of lubrication in both holes at the same time, depressing the plungers and filling me with cool gel. He doesn't waste any time bringing the rods up, sinking the tips in. The sadistic bastard narrates each detail as the ends rest, unmoving, just inside my abused sex and anus.

"The smallest ball, for the rear, is a half inch across, the next is more than double that at an inch and a quarter, with the last coming in at two inches. That last one is going to hurt." His recital and warning has me ready to hyperventilate. I want to go home, and barring that, I want to go to bed. He blithely finishes his descriptions. "And that's the smaller side. The other rod sports balls half again of each in diameter, with the lengths of both at eight, insertable inches." He starts moving them inward without warning. Up and up they go until he reaches the first, but it's actually not bad so far. The rods themselves are maybe the diameter of my pinky. When he hits the first of the balls, they sink in easily, squeezing the area between my anus and vaginal opening as they pass through simultaneously. The next he goes slower, and the pinch is sharper, causing me to dread the final ones. These meet resistance, and he steadily holds pressure, drawing it out as that flesh in between is flattened, bringing about a burning pain that is inescapable.

Tears prick my eyes by the time they're finally seated fully. Marcus rocks it around, causing me to groan with discomfort. I feel insanely full right inside my openings. I relax my face from its grimace, blinking my eyes open, and realize Apollo is, yet again, almost in my crotch, just watching.

I glance around the room as Braeden withdraws his wet dick from Rex, leaving his ass hanging open and leaking a mess, slowly shrinking up after the massive invasion it has endured. I can only imagine I'm about to look the same down there. *What the hell, why hadn't Brade been wearing a condom?*

Rex and Braeden are both watching me now, and I close my eyes again in shameful, embarrassment. Marcus picks up a metal bullet vibrator that he clicks on. Running it around the edges of my openings, it turns some of the pain into pleasure. I moan, shifting my hips as much as the restraints allow. Apollo takes over teasing up and down my swollen flesh as Marcus withdraws the rods. The balls coming out together feel exquisitely overwhelming with the vibrations isolated under the hood of my clit. Apollo pokes the bullet in my ass when the rod has been removed, my sphincter closing over the vibrating intrusion, as he catches my clit in his teeth. He flicks his tongue on the captured nub, and I feel an impending orgasm rapidly approaching. He pulls the bullet out and lifts his head away. The two work in tandem— Marcus pushing the rod back in and pulling it out slowly, as Apollo repeats his actions with the bullet and sucking.

That's it for me. I cry out and my ass and pussy clench and pulse. Surprising Apollo with the intensity, the bullet sucks into my ass and Apollo dives in after it with his fingers. The pinch of pain along with the sudden intrusion bring on another round of spasms, making my whole body stiffen with the back-to-back orgasms. He pulls his fingers out and gives me a final lick to the clit before putting his tongue into my pussy, literally licking out the fluid I'd released. It's too much for my oversensitive pussy, and he finally relents.

Apollo sits up and pulls Marcus in for a sloppy kiss, tongues and teeth clashing, liberally sharing what he's collected. It's the hottest thing, the guys making out, not the weird oversharing. I'm fairly surprised at the intensity of the encounter with the man that seemed so cold before. He and Marcus are definitely lovers. I'm now curious if Apollo is the one that introduced him to this. Before I have much time to think on it, Apollo is walking away to the sink to wash up, and Marcus is unhooking me before he moves to release Rex.

I attempt to stand on wobbly legs as pins and needles spread over the unconfined limbs. I move like I've been beaten, and I feel like I have been too. My body hurts so badly, inside and out. Now that the excitement is over my ass feels overused and extremely sore. I can only sympathize with the guys though. I wasn't used quite so harshly as they were. The beginnings of a headache are putting painful pressure behind my eyes, and my mouth is extremely dry. Rex looks as rough as I feel and is walking very gingerly while Marcus ushers us to the door.

"I'll be in here cleaning up. All of you go get washed up and rest. There are painkillers in the kitchen area above the sink and in the hall closet. There's also some numbing cream you may want to use for some relief. Get your rest, we have a showing tonight for prospective buyers of Three and Four, but since you're all being trained together, you'll be shown together." I'd assumed it was night already, but with no clocks or windows it made it difficult to judge the time. I actually have no idea how long it's been since we were taken. I would guess four or five days, but that's only because of the length of the leg and underarm hair I had declined to shave. I'm sort of embarrassed about that now. "It's morning now," he says, seeing the confusion on our faces. He looks at a watch I hadn't really noticed before but has to push something on the side to make it light up. "A little past nine. I brought you in around five. You did well for the first portion, but the rest won't be so easy." He gives an asshole smirk with the parting shot.

Easy my aching ass. Fucking twat.

8

AN EMBARRASSING REALITY

We slowly make our way out of the room. The guys offer me the shower first, and I don't even pretend to argue about it. I shower as quickly as I can, considering the state of my muscles, and tenderness of other parts. They were nice enough to let me go first and are in similar conditions. I gently wash between my legs, and the cloth comes back with streaks of pink. I'm not surprised, but hope I don't have to be touched down there before it heals. I get out and wrap up in my towel, heading straight for the bedroom. I don't want to make any of the guys wait to get clean for me to dress in there.

Braeden is up next and gives me a wan smile as he passes me on his way into the bathroom. I slide more clothing on under my towel in case the others walk in. Not that they haven't seen literally every part of me now, but I feel more modest outside that room. For some reason I wasn't as hesitant as I'm feeling now. I drink most of a bottle of water before I come up for air and get started on the tangles in my hair with the brush I'd found in the mirrored cabinet. Rex and Emmett come in as Braeden is coming out, and I can't look at any of them as Emmett speaks to Brade.

"Hey, man. I found Tylenol and ibuprofen. Which would you rather?" Braeden takes one of the bottles and shakes some tablets out before handing them over to me. I get up to grab the other bottle too and shake out two of each. Smarties should know you can take both of those together, even if it's not great for you, and I'm taking advantage of that fact. I say as much when all three complain about mixing them. Instantly, they're all taking two of whatever they already hadn't, and I can't keep a giggle from slipping out. They just looked so desperate for it. "I also found this in the cupboard. I'm going to shower, and I'll leave it in the bathroom, I saw gloves on the back of the toilet." Waving the tube at us, now red in the face, Emmett goes into the bathroom and closes the door behind him.

"Birdie baby, how are you doing?" Braeden comes to hold me, easing us both down on the bed.

Burying my head in his chest I mumble, "Like I got fucked for hours and then managed to get road rash up my ass at the end." He chuckles before groaning at the jarring movement. I peek up and see Rex shifting from foot to foot, trying to get comfortable.

Soon, the water shuts off, and a few moments later, a yelp sounds out from behind the bathroom door. Rex rushes to it, and since none of the rooms other than that torture chamber we were in earlier have locks, he barges right in.

I wish he had knocked first. I'm for sure Emmett wishes he had knocked first. He's holding his rear, his gloved-up hand between his legs. I look away as soon as it registers what I'm seeing.

"Get the fuck out, Rex! Ever hear of privacy, or knocking? For fucks sake, shut the door!" Poor Emmett is horrified.

"Sorry, man. Thought you fell or something." Rex is mortified. I've noticed we're all avoiding certain topics like they're the plague, which is odd to me considering none of us objected much at all while it was happening.

Emmett's voice comes muffled through the door, "I didn't know it was going to sting. I should have realized, although now that it's been a minute, it's feeling better." He opens the door dressed and acting like nothing has happened at all. The federal agent façade is firmly in place. Rex takes his turn, and the shower starts again. Emmett looks from me to Braeden and then walks out of the bedroom without a word.

In the quiet of the water being turned off, a muffled curse comes through the door. A few moments later, Rex comes out walking almost normally. I guess the stuff must work if he can stand straight without grimacing. He also leaves the room and closes the door behind him. Braeden rubs my back then sits back to look at me.

"Why don't you go try some?" I don't want to tell him that I'm hurt. It's not bad, but if the guys had a bad time, and I'm assuming they don't have my issue, I don't want to know how it will feel with scuffed up, open spots.

"I think I'm alright. The painkillers are helping." He looks at me like he knows there's something else but decides not to pursue it. Gently, he sits me down on the bed and goes into the bathroom. I don't hear anything until the sink turns on, then he comes back out with a glove and a tube in his hand.

"If you won't do it yourself, I will. It's instant relief." I shake my head no. "Then drop 'em." He better not mean what I think he does.

"I'm not letting you do that. You're my best friend!" I'm shocked that he would want to. Not that he wouldn't want to take care of me, but that he'd go so far to do so.

"I've had my dick in your mouth, we've seen each other naked, I've fucked, been fucked, and I'm sure, will watch you get fucked. I think I can apply some medication for you." He forgot to add fucking me too, or maybe he left that out on purpose.

"I can't." I cross my arms and stare past him.

"Why not? Do you not trust me?" Now he looks hurt.

"I have some, um— abrasions." I say it as quietly as possible. He looks confused. "I'm afraid it will hurt them, they need to heal." Understanding dawns.

"How bad? Are you bleeding or just roughed up a little?"

"The washcloth was pink when I cleaned up." I'm mortified and don't want to discuss this.

"That fucker, he was too rough with you. Let me see."

"No, I'll be fine, it just needs a bit to heal up."

"You may not have that kind of time. I need to know how bad it is. I'm not new to accidental rear end injuries."

Fuck my life.

"Fine, but in the bathroom. I don't want the others to walk in." I get up carefully and go into the bathroom with Brade right behind me closing the door.

"Alright, easiest would be to lean over the sink." Without a word and my features as blank as possible, I drop my pants and bend over. Braeden gets on his knees behind me. My eyes well up when he parts my cheeks. This is not how it's supposed to be. "Just relax, little bird. It's only me." He wets a cloth in the sink and presses it against me. It's still slightly pink, but less than it was. "I think it's ok. I'm going to put some of this stuff on it. Take a deep breath. It only stings for a second." He puts it around my opening then slips a generous amount inside. My ass is on fire, but I was prepared for the sting and keep quiet. Thankfully, it doesn't take long before the discomfort dissipates. I refuse to think about Braeden touching me this way. We'll get out of here and never think of this again. He helps me with my pants and gets me back to bed, tucking me in. "I'll be back in a few minutes."

I lay there trying to sleep and just start crying, unable to stop my tears. I muffle it in my pillow, not wanting anyone else to hear me.

Braeden

I COME out of the bedroom to find Rex and Emmett talking. "Have they come out of there yet?" Rex answers me.

"Not unless there's another exit in there. Why?"

"I need to speak with them." I turn to head back to that room. I'm pissed and going to let those two jackasses know they can't treat my girl like they have.

"We're the contacts here. What do you need to speak to them about?" Emmett this time. Acting like the usual stuck up prick he is. It really does ruin his attractiveness.

"That's not your business." I move to leave, but both men close ranks to block me. *Are they fucking kidding right now?* "You two are fucked up, you know that right? I didn't sign up for this shit." More quietly I add, "Neither did Lark, and she's hurt, I need to go talk to them."

"What?!"

"How?" I shush them. Lark will have my balls if she knows I tattled.

"Be quiet, she didn't want anyone to know. I finally made her let me look. It's not terrible, but she needs time to rest and let it heal. They were too rough with her." They both look concerned, then Rex addresses me.

"Rough with her? How bad is it? You tore my shit up, but I'm alright." I blow out a breath, trying to keep my patience with the neanderthal, so I can attempt to explain in words he'll understand.

"That was my dick, and I was more careful than you realize. For Lark's sake, not yours," I'm quick to assure him. "I just need to go let them know she needs to be left out of whatever is going on later." With that, I push through them, and they don't stop me this time. Instead, they follow. I reach the door as Marcus and Apollo are coming out.

"Gentlemen, may we help you?" Apollo addresses us, back to the professional businessman now.

"Lark needs to be left out tonight. She's bleeding some, not bad, but it needs a chance to heal," Emmett speaks up. I'm going to kick his ass. Always has to try to outdo everyone else. I have no clue why Rex puts up with him and claims him as his closest friend.

"I noticed some blood on the equipment. It wasn't much, but I was sending Dr. Martins to check on her anyway before you have to get ready. We'll see you later." Seemingly unconcerned, they both leave.

Shaking my head at their attitude, I go back into the bedroom to get some rest and find Lark crying. Climbing into her narrow bed behind her, I offer what comfort I can.

~

Lark

FEELING the bed dip and arms wrapping around me, I turn and bury my face in Braeden's chest, crying for quite a while longer. "I don't know why I did that! What is wrong with me?" I'm so confused and ashamed.

"We all did, Lark. You're not the only one. We're in a fucked up situation, and we need to do what we have to, to get out. If the situation was different, and we didn't know help was coming soon, we would be fighting every minute. Cooperation is our chance at surviving this. Fighting may get one, or all, of us killed." Even if he's right, it doesn't help my feelings of shame and disgust.

"But I told him he could go down on me when he asked! Why would I answer him? Tell him yes? That's not me." My venting does nothing to calm me and being so upset I start crying again.

"I'm not sure, but that room and the situation makes for a lot of trauma. Even if it doesn't seem like it in the moment. Do what they want, and we'll get out of here. Please don't cry any more, love bird." He holds me tighter, and I eventually fall asleep.

Rex

HEARING Lark crying is killing me, and I wish I could go hold her. Despite wanting to, I know I won't be welcome.

Going into the common area to speak with Emmett, I sit on one of the chairs and wince. Even with the meds and cream, my ass still feels like it took a beating. Who knew Braeden had such a big cock? Lark never said anything. I'll admit to being jealous of him before, but now I wonder, after seeing them interact in this scenario, if they ever thought about being together. The way he cares for her I could see it being a possibility. Trying to push those thoughts from my head, I concentrate on Emmett.

"Any ideas on how soon you think we can get out of here?" I ask him while doing stretches on the floor, trying to limber my muscles up. Doesn't hurt to stay ready for trouble.

"Nothing we haven't already discussed. Talking to Apollo about it more risks being overheard, just need to wait it out, I suppose. Although I didn't think we would be moving this quickly— something is off. We were picked up nearly a week early, and when it was originally discussed, there wasn't any physical stuff for almost two weeks until all the test results were in. Something has sped it up. I think we need to scrap this whole operation and get out of here while we still can. If we can't get an extraction for everyone approved, and soon, we need to see about breaking out ourselves." Emmett's concern and suspicions are enough to validate the bad feeling that's been burning in me since we woke up with Lark.

Having nothing productive to add, I just agree with him. Then a thought occurs, something that's been bugging me. "Hey, um, I was wondering. Did you feel off in there? Before, I mean? I feel like I was entirely too okay with what went down even if it's something we'd agreed to."

"I felt the same way, like coming down off a high. Maybe it's sensory deprivation or something with all the white, the lighting, and the plastic in there." While troubling, that's not enough to hold my attention when Emmett berates me. "You know, you should be in there with Lark, right?"

"I'm aware." I bite out. "Just as we're both also aware she'd probably kick me in the balls if I tried. Today was hard, watching her hate me, and sure as shit, it'll only get worse."

"She's a little firecracker in the sack, isn't she?" My eyes narrow on my best friend and housemate as he goads me. "I remember that one time coming home from an assignment and she was going to town on your dick. Kind of like she did Braeden's today."

Jaw tight, and quelling the urge to punch my partner in the face, I grit out, "What's your point, Emmett?" He's sporting a devious expression, and I'm thinking we might tussle yet.

"Just saying, man, if you're trying to push her straight into his arms you're doing an excellent job. You think he hasn't been waiting— for years— to have the opportunity to be her one and only? I know I wouldn't have passed it–" Emmett cuts himself off, features morphing into contriteness, but it's too late for that.

"Passed *what* up, Em? Taking my girl?" *Emmett wants Lark? I'll kick his ass.* He rises to the bait.

"Not your girl anymore, and what a bang-up job you did of taking a break with her so you could come here." He shakes his head as he waves his arm out to encompass the room, before changing the direction of the conversation slightly, away from dangerous territory. "Just saying that if for some reason you two didn't work out, I can't swear I wouldn't have tried to swoop in. As for Braeden, while he's outwardly gay— and I believe he really is at least to a point— have you ever noticed more than a hook up or friends with benes' around?"

Thinking back, I can't recall anyone long-term being around or mentioned. In fact..."I'd say the same about you. Why is it, Emmett, that you've not had a real girlfriend since I met Lark? And the one at the time disappeared rather quickly now that I think about it." My suspicions are confirmed by my friend's uncharacteristic bashfulness. Incredulous at my revelation, I continue, "Dude, are you hooked on my girl?" My world has gotten beyond wobbly, first having to break-up with Lark, then her getting mixed up in this, and now finding out my best friend, who may as well be family, has a torch for her. The sense of surreality is hard to take.

"Man, I can't believe it's taken you this long to notice. How the hell did you ever get her to date you? You have to be the luckiest son of a bitch that she did, and that we're like family; otherwise, I'd have had to take my chances." *What the hell? Emmett and Lark?*

"You never tried–" He cuts me off before I finish my accusation.

"Nah, man. She thinks I'm weird. Besides, she's hung up on you like crazy— or was. You need to figure it out as soon as we abort this shit show."

I'm in full agreeance with his advice— only figuring out the how part is going to be tricky with a pissed off Lark. Woman can hold a grudge, and it's not like my dumbass did something small like forgetting to put the lid back on the peanut butter or leaving the toilet seat up. Actually, it may have been close to when she fell in, in the middle of the night. The aftermath hadn't been pretty.

"Alright, bro. I get it, I'm wiped and ready for bed. See you when we get up?" Slightly dejected I leave Emmett, heading for the bedroom. Lark appears to be sleeping when I check on her, but as I go toward her for a closer look, I get stopped short by Braeden's arctic stare. Shaking my head at his alpha male display, I climb into my own bed.

"She'll eventually need you. She'll need both of us." Braeden's declaration is quiet. I don't acknowledge him, but he's right. I just need to get over my ego and pride right now.

9

MUTINY

Lark

Waking to my shoulder being shaken, I blink bleary eyes open to see Brade and start to smile at him until I remember where we are. He gives me a small smile in return.

"Hey, sleepy bird, it's time to get up and ready." He seems nervous. "I may have spoken with the guys so that I could tell Apollo that you need a timeout on all this. Him and Marcus just came in to get us ready for tonight. They brought the doctor along with them." He sees the horrified look on my face and quickly speaks before I do. "Rex and Emmett tried to stop me from talking to Apollo until I told them you weren't going to be at a hundred percent for a while. After that, they let me go talk to him, but he wanted a reason why, and I didn't see any way around it. He, or maybe Marcus, decided to bring the doctor. I'm sorry, I just don't want you hurt more." He looks like a kicked puppy. I want to be mad at him, but I know he was just trying to help.

"It's alright, Brade. I really would have been fine though," I gripe. I excuse myself to the bathroom, do my business and brush my teeth. At least I don't have to worry about a period while I'm here. Braeden and I have separate bathrooms at home, so other than PMS he doesn't have to deal with that sort of thing. Most women don't have them often on the shot, but I'm one of those weird ones that occasionally do. I brush my long hair out and put it up in a ponytail with a hair tie I found in the closet earlier. Going back out, I see Rex and Emmett have joined us.

"Braeden, you coming with me?" I ask, noticing the disappointed look on Rex's face when I don't acknowledge him. Braeden nods and follows me out of the room.

I'm turning into the common area when Braeden grabs my elbow, redirecting me back toward the 'white room' as I've dubbed it in my head. I pause, not wanting to go back in there, before giving in when Braeden nudges me again.

The door is unlocked when we reach it, and we go right in. Rounding the last corner I see Dr. Martins is setting some things out on the counter, and Apollo and Marcus are at a closet I didn't notice before. The door is flat without an obvious knob, but my curiosity flees as Dr. Martins speaks.

"Ms. Jones, I hear you have some rectal bleeding." *Oh, freaking kill me now. Did he have to say that out loud?*

Hoping to avoid this altogether, I try, "I suppose, but don't think it's enough to warrant a visit to the doctor."

"I disagree. You need to be in top shape for any presentations, or so I'm told, and you have your first one in a couple hours. I need to assess if you are well enough to participate. Is that the only area of concern?" I nod my head in the affirmative. "Then please remove the clothing from your lower half. Your companion can stay or go, that's your decision." *I don't want anyone here for this, even if it is just Braeden.*

"Brade, you can go. I'll be fine." He looks like he wants to disagree, but he just nods and tells me to let him know if he's needed. I'm not sure how to do that unless he's staying close, and, knowing him, he won't go far. I have a feeling this room is soundproof. After he leaves, I wait for the other two now standing closer and observing, to leave as well.

~

"Ms. Jones, please remove your clothing and get on the table," Dr. Martins directs me again.

"Aren't you two leaving?" I address Apollo and Marcus. Marcus answers for them both.

"No, we're not." No explanation, just a refusal.

My arms cross in defiance. I didn't want to do this in the first place. In response to my mutiny, Marcus comes towards me, stalking my retreating steps until my back hits the chair.

He flips me up on it and pins my arms. "Take them off, or I will." He's such a dick I know he'll do it. Glaring at him, I shimmy out of my pants and underwear. Dr. Martins comes up, now wearing a pair of green exam gloves, and places my feet in the stirrups. My knees are still closed, and he pushes the feet up and back to spread them. I want to close them again, but I suspect I'd just get restrained. I fume, refusing to look at anyone. Suddenly, the table under my bottom drops away leaving it hanging out in the air. Again. *Awesome, just awesome.* The doctor pulls a table with supplies over. Taking a piece of gauze and placing it against my sorest hole he tells me to bear down some as he swipes with the gauze. It must come back with some pink on it because the next thing I know I feel a cool wetness and something small and thin entering me. I jump and wiggle back.

"Hold still, please, Ms. Jones, so that I may finish what I am doing." A hint of irritation has entered his voice. *Fuck him and his snooty ass.*

"Next person to touch me without asking or even bothering to explain what needs to be done, doctor or not, I'm going to kick your ass. I've cooperated so far, even though I had to force myself to do it. I'm done. Explain or fuck off!" During my tirade I've pulled myself up and off the chair dislodging the implement. Marcus heads towards me with, I'm sure, the intent to put me back up there and restrain me, but he's going to be in for a big surprise if he touches me.

I make sure to keep the other two in my sight as I back away from him. He speeds up, impatient, and tries to grab me. Instead of pulling back, I step forward, swinging the fist opposite the arm he went for. With his lunge forward and my abrupt change of direction, along with his height, he sets me up for the perfect throat punch. There's the sound of flesh on flesh, then Marcus is bent over retching, holding his abused throat. Apollo and the doctor look pissed.

I open the first drawer I reach and grab blindly, coming out with a handful of metal balls. I start launching them and hit Apollo in the face. The doctor has ducked behind one of the chairs. The next drawer holds two coiled whips. Normally a person would have a fifty-fifty chance to wield them correctly. But I dated a circus performer one summer and traveled with him, let's just say Braeden didn't approve. He happened to be the guy with the whips, and I got to be the girl with the cigarette in her mouth. Apollo speaks to me.

"Now, Lark, put those down before you hurt yourself." He holds his hands up like he means no harm, but it's too late for that.

I smirk and coil one whip over my left shoulder and transfer the other to my left hand. I'm accurate with both hands with a whip, but throw better with my right. Opening the next drawer while Marcus is still bent double, trying to breathe, reveals batteries wrapped in groups with cellophane. I grab a package of four D batteries and chuck them at Dr. Martins' head as he's trying to circle around the room to get behind me, but he ducks back to his position and narrowly avoids my makeshift missile.

"Lark, what the heck is going on?" At all the noise Braeden pops in, concern in his voice. Taking one look at the situation, he runs for the door. "Rex, get your ass in here!" I hear him yell a moment later.

During that time, I throw the rest of the D batteries and move on to the next drawer. So far I'm holding them off. I know I'll have to incapacitate them eventually or face getting caught. I'm not going down without one hell of a fight though. This drawer has big flexible dildos, and I indiscriminately throw them until I see a tray of glass dildos and large glass butt plugs that Braeden's ass would be hard pressed to take. *What the fuck is wrong with these people that they want to shove huge shit in people?*

I start launching the plugs first, and they explode into chunks all around the three very pissed off men in the room. As I throw the last one and grab a glass dildo that could double as a javelin, all three of my guys come running in. *My guys? I suppose so.* I shrug at my internal debate. Rex is half worried, half amused, Braeden bends over laughing his ass off at the scene, which I guess from the outside might be amusing, and Emmett is looking on in horror. *Pussy.*

Marcus has finally straightened up— he comes at me with murder in his eyes, trying to yell at me. He only gets out, "Bitch," in a horrible scratchy, croaky voice.

I swing the whip in warning, just grazing the jeans he has on. The tip splits the jeans, and he jumps back before I can do too much damage to the skin underneath. Apollo tries coming at me at the same time, and he gets the 'javelin' nearly in his face before blocking it with his forearm. It only slows him down for a moment, but it gives me enough time to unfurl the other whip and wrap it around his ankle in a quick strike. The instant it wraps, I give a yank and bring him down on his back with a thump. The whip slackens enough that I'm able to flick it loose. I keep it going in random movements around me to deter anyone else from trying anything while holding the other at the ready. The doctor goes to help Apollo up, but no one makes a move for me. Braeden has mostly calmed himself, and Emmett looks rather impressed now. Rex is the first to attempt to get me to surrender.

"Lark, honey," he starts as I throw a glare his way, then he rephrases. "Lark, please put the whips down so we can talk about this." He makes a move in my direction, and I flick the other whip towards him in warning. Braeden speaks up taking pity on them

"She knows how to use those, as she's shown you already, and she can keep this up for at least an hour. I don't think we have that kind of time right now." *Why does he have to be logical? Can't he see I'm in a standoff?* "Fire bird? Do you want to tell me why you're flashing everyone, swinging whips, and throwing, are those sex toys, at everyone?" I shake my head no. *I do not have anything to say to those dicks.* "Did someone hurt you?" Now he's angry and looking to the three men, who up until yesterday, were strangers. "Do I need to kick someone's ass, Lark?" *Uh oh, real name, he's pissed.* I shake my head again, figuring I'd better answer.

"They need to learn to ask permission before touching me. Whatever ambiguity this room imbued earlier isn't working this time. I care. A lot." Apollo has gotten up and gestures for everyone to back up.

"Lark, we really don't have time for this. I won't punish you for defending yourself in here, but if we're late and marked up in ways we can't easily explain, I can't protect any of you. I apologize for our forwardness. Can we please finish up and prepare for the evening?"

Reasonable. Why is he reasonable now?

I slow the whips. "If you promise not to touch me without permission again, any of you, you have a deal." He nods his head in assent and I drop the whips.

"Marcus, get this cleaned up. Brent, come, let's finish checking her out before we're late." He must notice the shitty look Marcus gives him. "Marcus, if you hadn't tried to manhandle her, this may have all been avoided. And don't forget how the injury occurred in the first place. Although, I blame myself as well, as I should have paid more attention. I apologize for being distracted. I'll monitor more closely from now on."

I nod to my guys and make a shooing motion with my hand. They linger a moment, then turn and leave. I move back to the chair, and surprisingly it doesn't have anything I threw on it. I climb up and cross my arms.

"Relax, Ms. Jones. I'll explain everything before I do it and give you an opportunity to object." He washes his hands and gloves up, while Apollo brings him a newly stocked tray. "I need to irrigate the rectum, just enough to disinfect it to prevent infection. It's not an enema, and I won't use that much liquid. It uses a small tube that may feel odd, but should not be painful. If you feel any pain, let me know immediately." I don't object, and a basin is moved below me. I'm just going to ignore this as much as possible. Lubrication is applied, and the tube inserted a short way. I feel cool liquid pumped in, and it soothes the skin in there. After it's removed, the doctor explains his next steps. I have to evacuate the liquid now. *Of course I do.* I do so in mortification. It was a little pink, but he thinks it's okay. He wants to use an anal dilator, which is a smaller speculum essentially, so he can visually check. I'm not into this one, but he explains he'll numb my sphincter first. *I wish he would shut up, why did I want everything explained again?* He uses a numbing lube, and while he waits on that to take effect, he checks my vagina then probes around inside, every so often asking if anything hurts. Sore yes, hurt no. After that he applies the dilator. It doesn't hurt, but I can still feel it, and even more so when he clicks it open a few notches. He shines a light in and decides it's more chafing than anything from the lube wearing off. They decide to evaluate what they've been using and check to make sure they're all long-lasting formulas. Anything strictly water-based will absorb too quickly, he explains. With that finished, I'm done and get dressed.

"I suggest to be on the safe side that anal penetration is avoided for the next couple days. That could easily get worse," Dr. Martins addresses Apollo and Marcus, who have finished the clean up now. They nod their agreement, thank the doctor, and ask him to send the guys in on his way out. I stand there, waiting, for what, I'm not sure. Maybe an apology from Marcus. Not that he gives me one.

As the guys come in, Marcus instructs me to go shower and shave everything and threatens to do it himself if I don't. I leave to do so, knowing he'll make good on his threat.

~

Braeden

"Is LARK OKAY?" It's the first thing I want to know when she's gone. Apollo answers me.

"Yes, just have to avoid any backdoor activities for a couple days, only to be safe." He adds on the last to reassure me, I think. "We have a showing tonight. It's at my father's request, or I would have attempted to decline. Unfortunately, even I cannot defy Robert without consequence. Normally, you would all be outfitted, but I think some well-placed objects will help deter anyone from attempting to touch. There are usually one or two that will try anyway, but less is more in this case, in reference to clothing. I'll leave the rest to Marcus and see what I can find for Lark." With that, he leaves us with Marcus to take over.

10

THE SHOWING

We're all given an oil to rub down with before wide leather chokers with a ring on them are buckled around our necks, decent sized plugs are inserted, and clamps with feathers on the ends are put on our nipples. I don't know why I'm surprised at the hoopla after earlier, but it seems a bit much. Especially, when a length of silk wraps around our dicks after we get them hard, and our balls are tied up to them with rings in an effort to decorate the display and help us stay erect for the showing. "Really, dude? Is this necessary?"

Marcus, of course ignores me and continues instructing us on how to place the material. The silk goes around our thighs and weaves up to our waists, criss-crossing our chests, and is twisted apart in the back to help hold our cheeks open to show off the plugs. A longer clamp is used on our perineum after it is pinched to shape it.

"Rex, I swear to fuck, if you ever get me involved in something like this again, I'll kick your ass out of the house." Emmett is not amused at the clamp.

In his defense, that part was the least fun besides the

degrading little bells hanging from it, jingling with every step. As we're finished off with our hands bound by our wrists behind our backs, Lark comes in. She stops dead in the middle of the floor, gaping. I'm embarrassed we look like harem rejects.

Lark

Holy buff babies. The guys are decked out and wrapped up like a dominatrix's wet dream. After earlier, I wouldn't have thought it possible, but I actually get a little excited looking at them. My pleasant view is interrupted when Marcus approaches and speaks to me for the first time since calling me a bitch.

"Four, if you would please disrobe and get in the chair, I can get you done quickly. The sooner you're ready, the less time everyone must be adorned this way. I'll explain what I'm doing as much as I can, there's always the chance we might be observed. I apologize for not doing it in the first place. You're being a good sport when you could have ratted us out. We took a chance going to the FBI for help when Rex started poking around looking for his friend and we appreciate both your, and Braeden's assistance." *Who's this and where is Marcus?* "And princess, don't think I have forgotten I owe you one," he says with a smirk. *And there he is, folks.* Braeden and Rex both start to object. I'm not sure what they think they're gonna do while tied up though.

Before they get far, Marcus the Douche speaks again. *Maybe I should call him Mad Dog. Code for Marcus the Douche.* I like the idea. "Speak out of turn, and I will use a gag— one that I can stick my dick in, and you don't want something that can accommodate my size in your mouth. That would be tame compared to the things Robert will do to you if you embarrass him." He shudders, as if recollecting past horrors, before continuing, "Three, you may be equinely inclined and hang lower, but I'm wider. Who wants to find out first?" No one responds. *Ohhh, I guess the glass plugs did have a use other than just being obscene. Ouch...*

I'm kinda confused as I was under the impression that the four of us as trainees would be interacting exclusively, at least for now. *I need to talk to Rex or Emmett ASAP.* Right now there isn't time as Apollo joins us and hands a tray to Marcus. I sigh, strip, and climb in the chair yet again. I'm gonna have my name stenciled on it if we don't get out of here soon.

"Apollo has cobbled some things together to be a place-keeper. Essentially, a decoration. Dr. Martins has approved it as well. Are you alright with me going ahead? You can take a look at the tray to see that it all resembles what the others are wearing. Except a couple, being you have different parts." I glance over and quickly away, nodding my head.

After gathering my dark hair high onto my head in a secure bun, Apollo, much to my surprise, starts applying makeup. Marcus has a miniature looking plug that's made of what seems to be silicone and is missing the big part. It only has the flare on the outside portion and a small, open end that is inserted that expands enough to hold it in place. I close my eyes and try to relax, pretending I'm at a perverted spa and that I didn't notice what Marcus is holding.

I peek when I feel Apollo step back and see Marcus ready for his part. He inserts the contraption first into what looks like a mini tampon applicator, before I'm lubed up, then, with a sharp gasp from me at the rubbing on the damaged tissue, the tube is pushed in, and the insert is released. It's not terrible, but I can tell it's there, as I'm still really sore. I suppose anything at all would still be noticeable.

"I'm going to put extra numbing lube in with a syringe attached to a tube, then I'll do the same to you all, minus the lidocaine, since I'm not sure how long we'll be or when I can re-up it. All the plugs you have are equipped with removable cores, so I can periodically apply more." The tube is longer than the funnel like plug, and it goes in higher. As Marcus backs it out, he releases its contents. It definitely has more of that numbing stuff as I feel more relaxed almost instantly. Holding onto the funnel sleeve, he inserts a rod that snaps into place with a hollow bulb hanging on the outside mimicking a large plug. It's an ingenious design. *Might have to give Sunny boy props.*

Before finishing me, he goes and tops off the guys too while Apollo dusts my body in gold powder and wraps me in a silk ribbon that matches what the others are in. *Not sure how I feel about this collar though. Mostly claustrophobic at this point.*

Marcus comes back and applies clamps to my nipples, clit, and taint using a side clamp that only goes into my vagina and tightens down from there and the outside. I squirm at all the hardware. Then comes the dildo, a silicone piece could be the javelin's shorter twin. I'm dry down there, so Marcus applies enough lube to grease a pig before working the mini javelin in until it's finally inside completely. After he cleans up, he attaches a harness he fashioned out of more ribbon looped through the ring on the end to hold it in. *Walking is going to be a bitch.* The guys' eyes are all full of heat, including Apollo and Marcus, when I look around. Marcus basically lifts me and places me standing up to avoid bending. I thank him, truly, and attempt to walk normally after them out of the room and through the apartment. Being nervous about others seeing me naked and adorned in such a manner, I get between Rex and Braeden, and surprisingly, Emmett gets behind me. They've effectively put me inside a circle.

Guards fall into position all around us as we go into the hall. We're led through the commons, down a ramp covered in industrial carpeting, and into a small ballroom with a circular stage set in the middle of a horseshoe-shaped table. Mostly men, and a couple women, are already seated with their plates of food. *Is this a fucking dinner party?* The room is done in red and black, not a blood red, but more of a burgundy. Low lighting keeps it looking mysterious, but carefully placed spotlights illuminate certain areas. We're taken over to a wall in the shadows, but off to the side. It's slightly inset, so we are out of the way as we hug our backs to the surface. The temperature in the room isn't cold, but it's cool enough to make me shiver at the contact from the painted concrete. Apollo and Marcus take the empty chairs directly in front of us. I try to keep the surprise off my face when I see naked men and women only wearing red collars serving food and drinks. The people at the table reach out and touch them occasionally as they pass near, but the servers are impassive about it and continue on with their duties. A mixed group of men and women with leashes attached to their white collars are led in. I'm seeing a theme of colors here. Now, just to figure out what they mean. As the eating dwindles, and the drinking intensifies, the dishes are removed, and the servers thin out. An older man that greatly resembles Apollo claps his hands, drawing everyone's attention to him.

This must be Robert Vitti, Apollo's father. The light comes up a little, and I see Dr. Martins is sitting next to Marcus. I notice movement under the table, and, focusing on it, I see women are servicing some of the men. One of the women at the table also has her legs draped over another's shoulders and her chair is made differently than the others, it's missing a section of the seat and taller so that the woman with her head in her skirt is nearly a part of the furniture, allowing her to sit almost normally. She's paying attention to Mr. Vitti, acting like nothing is happening.

"I'd like to welcome you all to celebrate my son's first undertaking with a group of trainees. He has been invited to present them tonight. At his request, and his clients' demands, this will be observation only. No touching. The pets that have been brought in wearing the white collars are available for general use. The servers will pass out containers with equipment in case you feel the urge to play with your pet. To kick off the evening, two of my own will provide entertainment. If any others have brought something interesting, tell your server, and they will pass it on to me to make a decision."

Two masked women come in, stripping their robes off before they climb on the stage. Someone, I'm not sure who, activates a circular section that rises out of the center with a shallow step surrounding it.

It's like a display you see on game shows. I shiver at the thought of people probably being sold as merchandise on this very stage. My breathing picks up as I begin to panic. *What if we're being sold tonight? Can we really trust Apollo?*

Braeden scoots a foot, so it's touching mine, trying to comfort me. I'm afraid if I look at him I'll burst into tears again. I try to stare straight ahead so as not to bring attention to myself or my freak-out, but my only options are the naked slaves around the room or the guests at the table. Dr. Martins is in my line of sight enough for him to make eye contact, and his own widen at my growing distress. He surreptitiously gets Marcus' attention while the others select their 'pets'. *I won't be a fucking pet.*

Marcus leans in, speaking into Apollo's ear, too quietly for me to hear despite being right behind them. Apollo's shoulders stiffen slightly, and he jerks his head in a short nod. Marcus gets up from his seat to grab a black leather case out from under the table. He pulls a syringe out of it, and I begin to tremble. No one is commenting or even taking particular notice, making me think this is a normal occurrence. And maybe it is. He palms it and opens a square alcohol packet, shaking his head at Braeden's movement when he tries to step in front of me.

He whispers, "It's only a low dose of a very mild sedative. It'll take the edge off and get you through. I know you don't trust me, so think of it like this. No one here wants to see a dead fish up there, so it would do no good for me to knock you out." While his words are cruel, he does have a point, and I shakily nod my head.

Marcus turns me to get access to my inner elbow. He doesn't even untie my hands, just stretches my arm out, putting an uncomfortable pressure on my shoulder. The prick of the needle is over quickly, and moments after he pulls it out and puts a small bandage over the mark, I feel a calmness course through me.

Either I'm a lightweight, or the medication is stronger than he said. At this point I don't really care either way. I slump back against the wall, staggering a little. Brade and Rex both make low rumbling noises on either side of me, and Marcus shushes them. I lift my heavy-lidded eyes to stare at him. He mouths 'fuck' and turns a furious glare at the doctor. *Someone's in trouble.* The words sing in my head, giving me the urge to giggle. The sound catches Robert's attention.

"Is there something amusing to your female trainee that we should be aware of?" *Oh, shit. That's not good.* I try to school my expression and hope it doesn't look as idiotic as it feels on my face.

"No, Father. I believe the fault lies with the medication as sometimes happens. You know how these things go. Can't always predict a reaction. She won't need them soon enough when I'm finished training her." Apollo smooths over my faux pas, and while I'd like to be annoyed with him, I'm grateful for the redirection. Even as I'm angry, I'm having a hard time keeping my thoughts in order.

"Very well. Be sure she improves, or she'll need to be cut out of your venture." The men on either side and in front of me stiffen at the threat. They all remain quiet though, only Apollo nodding his head in the affirmative at his Father. "Let's get on with the show, shall we?" I turn my wandering attention to the stage along with everyone else not occupied in the room.

The first woman, a brunette with large breasts and darker skin climbs up on the dais on all fours. The other woman with smaller breasts and black hair has nearly the same skin tone and both are sporting pleasantly neutral expressions. They're both free of hair other than what's on their heads as far as I can tell.

The woman still standing opens a compartment in the stage floor and pulls out a couple of small packages and a pump bottle of what I'm assuming is lubricant. After placing it next to the kneeling woman, and stepping up on the ledge surrounding it, the dais slowly begins to rotate. The woman standing abruptly leans over, sticking her face between the other's thighs, and starts licking her from front to back in broad strokes. After a whole rotation, which I'm gonna guess is for everyone to get a good look, she spreads the woman open further, diving into her pussy, licking and sucking with a vengeance. Retreating after a few moments, her mouth and chin glistening, covered in her own saliva and vaginal excretions, she reaches for and opens one of the packages, removing a glove. Pulling it on, it goes up past her elbow. She does the same with the next package, donning purple nitrile gloves a doctor would use, but long enough to be opera length.

I look around some and notice the guys are glued to the scene as is most everyone else. I'd like to call them perverts, but even I'm intrigued by the women. Everyone else, that is, except Marcus and surprisingly, Dr. Martins. Instead, the heated desire reflected in his eyes is directed at me. *Well, that is decidedly unprofessional.* I shiver and not in disgust. *What is wrong with me? Is Stockholm syndrome setting in already?*

I turn my attention back to the women, trying to ignore my discomfort. My arms and shoulders are already getting sore from being bound, not to mention all the other issues I have going on. There's a box on the platform now as well, but I can't see what's in it from here. The standing woman pushes the other one's front down until her chest and head are resting on the surface, leaving her back end in the air. She taps the insides of her thighs, getting her to widen them until both holes are clearly visible. Several large screens flick on around the room before a video feed pops up. It's a close up from behind the kneeling woman with just a section of the other showing. This place is definitely set up for voyeurs, fucking pigs. I would think differently if this were consensual, but I seriously doubt that's the case. Some of the guests are getting antsy with the wait, shifting around in their seats. Finally, the standing woman starts the real spectacle.

Pumping lubricant in her gloved hands, she rubs it up and down her arms, coating them fully, and I begin to suspect what's happening. More lube is rubbed all over the woman's entrances, yet more on the two fingers that are pressed into the woman's vagina as the other hand uses forefinger and thumb to hold the edges of the hole wide for the camera.

With the noises from under the table being audible enough for cover and all the attention on the stage, I take a chance on kicking Rex. He's entirely too fixated on the scene. Broken up or not, he's pissing me off. And since I can feel angry again, I'm hoping I'm metabolizing the drug in my system. He narrows his eyes in my direction, and I give him an unfriendly sneer to convey my displeasure at him. When he turns his attention back to the stage, I go to kick him again, harder this time, except the quiet snap of Marcus' fingers halts my motion. With a huff, I return my own attention to the goings on.

There are two small fingers thrusting in and out of the woman making squishing noises I'm embarrassed to witness. The fingers withdraw, collecting more gel from the bottle, and re-enter with an extra one added. I try to ignore the squelching of all that liquid as the hand works rapidly, banging hard in and out until a fourth finger joins in. The hand is small, but the flesh is stretched out now, no longer requiring the fingers to hold it open for viewing. The other hand reaches under, pinching the clit and earning a moan from the woman as her pussy is simultaneously fondled and penetrated from behind. Turning her hand down, and improving the viewing angle for the camera that must be somewhere on the platform surface, the thumb tucks into the palm of her hand. It all gathers together and slowly pushes in, getting hung up at the widest part of the base of the thumb. It stops there, and the other hand collects more lube, slicking it all over the partially encased appendage and up to the elbow. Smoothing some up with the thumb of the free hand, the digit rubs ever-tightening circles over the anus. The tight ring spreads open with pressure, and the thumb slips all the way in and holds there. The lower hand starts twisting at the wrist, rotating in the vaginal opening and sliding forward, gaining ground while constant moans come from the stuffed woman. As the platform rotates, her face comes into view. Her cheek is resting on its side, eyes closed with tendrils of sweaty hair escaping the mask and pleasure and pain alternating on the features I can see.

I watch the monitor closest to me and see the hand sink in to the wrist. It slowly pulls back out, collecting more gel in the cupped palm before entering again in the thumb up position this time. I'm hoping they throw that bottle out when they're through here. I shudder at the thought of it being used again.

Due to the previous stretching, the hand slips in fairly easily now. The arm is rotated back and forth, presumably coating her walls with the slick gel, moving in and out quicker and quicker each time. The last time it comes out it's folded into a fist, and when it enters again, it keeps that form. It hits the opening and pauses there until slowly, the edges start creeping over knuckles with the constant pressure. It's not long before it sinks fully back in. Up until now the hand hasn't passed the wrist. That's no longer the case as it moves in further, almost halfway up the forearm before retreating. The arm picks up speed with just half of the fist coming out now, the grunts and moans picking up in speed and volume until she sounds like she's going to come.

Abruptly, the fist pops out, and only three fingers enter back in, curling back to face the rear. The thumb in her ass pulls out, returning with a finger to settle on either side of the entrance to press outward. The hole continues to spread open until the fingers in the vagina push the tissue out and down toward the anal opening. Spread from the outside and pressed from the inside, the pink flesh slightly protrudes from the hole. A tongue appears on screen and begins licking that flesh, poking it back in as the fingers push it out in an obscene display. Full lips seal over it, sucking, drawing out an almost wail from the woman being worked over. *If that actually feels that good, I might want to try it.*

I shift my gaze away from the monitor, ashamed at my thoughts the women have inspired. I see the doctor dividing his attention between watching the show and glancing at me. When he notices me looking, he licks his lips purposefully. *Would he do that if I sat on his face?* I shake the thought of me and the perverted doctor engaging in any sexual act from my head and go back to watching the monitor. Well, I try to anyway. Robert must have been watching our group instead of the 'show' as he calls a halt to it, causing the ladies to literally freeze their positions.

"Apollo, is your cousin permitted to use your female?" His tone is all innocence, but the predator peeks out of the pleased mask through his eyes.

I try not to show any reaction, and from the silence next to me, the guys are doing the same. Thankfully, Apollo shoots that down with a curt, "No."

He seems to debate for a moment before signaling Marcus,

who turns and pulls me down under the table and pushes me between Apollo's legs. I let out a squeak from the toys shifting at the abrupt movement.

Preempting my inclination to balk at servicing him, Apollo pulls me up and into his lap. "I'd rather her mouth be fresh for her show." He doesn't give any further explanation, and the awkwardness of moving around has my shoulders getting all my attention from the strain in them as well as pushing the dildo uncomfortably against my cervix.

As if sensing my discomfort, Apollo parts his legs to get the pressure off my nether regions and uses a hand to rub my shoulders, occasionally straying over my chest, but I ignore that figuring it's part of the act.

Robert gives the signal to resume, and my gaze eventually moves to one of the monitors to see what's going on with the women on the stage when my curiosity wins out.

The mouth is gone, and the drenching of the lube is happening again. In this case I have to agree with the excessive use of it. Quickly, much more so than with the vagina, fingers are pressed, one after the other, into the tightest hole. Within a few short minutes, the hand is curled and trying to move past the widest part. The other hand enters the vagina with two fingers, and the skin around the hand in the ass bulges out in spots. The fingers in the vagina are actually pushing the sphincter over the ones in the back from the other side, making the hand slide in to the wrist. The woman in panting now and squeals when the digits pull out of her pussy and her clit is manipulated by them. The hand is left in the back end, while the other gets a vibrating bullet from the box and applies it to the clit. The wrist withdraws, now ending in a fist, and is worked in and out and pushed nearly to the elbow and back rapidly. The arm withdraws fully, and the glove is stripped off it, discarded into a previously unnoticed bin. A long black glove is pulled from a newly opened package, and it covers all the way up to the standing woman's shoulder.

~

I SQUIRM a little and feel the dildo shift in me. If I squeezed my legs together and rocked enough, with this show going on, I could probably get off. My attention, briefly diverted from the show, is pulled to the papers Robert had slid to the man next to Apollo. Surreptitiously, I shift under the guise of getting more comfortable. Really, my ass is done, so it's not all made up.

My wiggling has done what the ladies started, and Apollo is firm enough to be poking me with his stiffy. It's kismet that he needs to readjust to get comfortable, and he stands me between him and the man with the papers. Taking advantage of my bindings and environment, I keep my head bowed and eyes downcast. I can see the top page, and I'm not amused— it's a struggle not to kick Apollo.

According to what I'm able to read before the man flips to the next one, the woman on the funky chair is the one buying Rex and Emmett, while the other patrons are here to view Brade and me. We are listed on the paperwork along with our attributes. All with Apollo named as the trainer and broker. *I swear to fuck, if he sells us tonight, I will geld him.*

My moment is over, and I only catch a glimpse of what looks to be a proposal for Apollo to take over a shipping route. Whether it's people, drugs, or something else, I don't get to find out before I'm resituated on Apollo's lap and directed to watch the women again.

I acquiesce yet stay determined to find out more of what's going on. Focusing back on the women, I find the lady standing has her fingers entering back into the woman's ass. She sinks them completely, then the hand, past the wrist and to the elbow. Pulling back a few inches then pressing forward again further than before, the whole arm is worked in. The woman being fisted is trembling and panting incessantly. The bullet is introduced again, and within a few moments, the woman is almost approaching orgasm from the noises she makes. Reaching into the endless box of tricks once more, an apparatus is pulled out and quickly secured to hold the bullet on the clit to free the other hand up to go right back into her pussy. With the vibrator and the intense anal and vaginal stimulation, the woman's orgasm crashes over her, drawing hoarse screams from her throat.

The pace doesn't stop, her pussy clearly clenching around the wrist and the anus spasming on the arm lodged in her ass. The hand in the vagina comes out covered in fluid. The vibrator stops, but the arm in the rear continues moving, the other hand reaching for another object. A dildo, with raised nubs protruding from it, is turned on, making it vibrate. It sinks in deep, and it and the arm are working in tandem. The toy, outpacing the arm, is contacting hard enough to echo through the room. On a final stroke, it's buried to the hilt, holding deep. I hear the vibration increase in intensity, and the tongue appears again, licking that stretched skin around the edges of the rear hole, I'm not even sure how she can feel it at this point. *Probably more for the engrossed audience's benefit.* The woman begins moaning insanely. *She's really going to get off again?*

A few moments later, the woman does just that. Coming as the toy is withdrawn, her pussy starts squirting from the strength of the orgasm. The woman's legs partially give out as the hand is removed. The standing woman slips her gloves off while the camera view refocuses on the anus until it slowly contracts, unable to quite close all the way after the abuse it just took. Two servant men appear to carry her out, while the other helps clean up the stage before slipping away. I hear more than one groan around the room while all this takes place.

From the expressions on some of the guests, they are climaxing themselves. When I take a good look, I notice several have servants on the table filling their pussies, asses, or both with toys, continuing their own show.

Is this how I'll be if we don't get out of here? A pet that follows commands? I shudder at the thought, this time keeping my composure. I just need to comply and finish watching this insanity.

11

TRAIN WRECK

A clapping sounds out, and I realize it's Robert, and that I've gotten distracted from the business dealings again. It's only been about forty-five minutes, I estimate, that we've been here even though it feels like hours. I'm ready to leave and corner Apollo for some answers, but my wishes are thwarted when Mr. Vitti stands to address the room.

"A fine display from two of my ladies. Now, we have the pleasure of my son's presentation to enjoy. Son, would you like to say a few words before you get started?" His tone of voice is jovial, but the look on his face is almost evil. I shiver, afraid of ever attracting his attention directly or ending up with him alone. Marcus gets me up to stand back by the guys as Apollo stands to speak.

"Change of plans, Four," Marcus whispers, "to stop the chance of you being pulled in by any of the others, you're going to be the main attraction. Just keep your eyes on us, and you'll get through it fine." He looks at me with sympathy. What could have happened that I was going up there alone? As we make our way over, another servant is finishing up using a disinfectant on the platform. I'm glad it's clean, that last chick made a hell of a mess. I stumble when I hear Apollo start speaking.

"As our trainees have just begun, we're going for an old-fashioned train ride instead of anything too exotic. This is about to be a seven-way party. Feel free to blow your own load as you watch." With a smarmy smile, he meanders over to the group. Marcus begins quietly giving directions. I tell myself to breathe. It's almost over. *Wait, did he say SEVEN? Who the fuck are the other three?*

He unties my hands and helps me up then onto my back to lie on the raised dais. My gold dusted shoulders and arms hurt from being bound so long, and everything that touches me is picking up the sheen. Motioning me to lift my rear end, a wedged cushion slips under my hips. Marcus leaves me be for a moment while he sets out tubes of lubrication and has the guys bend over. He empties them one by one, through the holes in their plugs after the core is removed and spreads it around by grabbing the base and twisting it— causing groans to sound in succession. Apollo joins us, kneeling before me to loosen the ribbon holding the dildo. He carefully slides one of the tubes in me next to it and spins the toy as he presses the plunger to work the slick around. It instantly feels better, although I don't think I was dry after watching the show, very much the opposite had been happening. Maybe it's for sound effects and not to make things slide easier.

I notice the screen come to life as the scene gets started. *I guess we're jumping right in then.* Apollo lowers his head and starts licking everything between my legs, sucking my lips and clit into his mouth and nibbling around. The clamp is still on, and it's not a very intense sensation when he sucks on it, from lack of blood flow. *How long can clamps stay on without damage?* I realize I have an excellent view of what is now a split screen. One half of the picture is of between my legs and the other of my head and upper body, and I still can't figure out where the cameras are. I look up as a penis enters the monitor screen in my line of sight. Tipping my head back, I find it's attached to the doctor. The very nude doctor. *I'm going to get fucked by him, too?* He looks at me with the desire from earlier that now makes so much sense. *He fucking knew what was about to happen.* He rubs the head of his dick over my lips, and I tip my head back further, determined to put on a good enough show that Apollo's father will leave us alone. *Screw them all if they think this will break me.* I grab an ass cheek in each hand, open my mouth wide and take him in to the hilt, swallowing as he hits my throat. He grunts in surprise, and I hold him there, sucking hard. My fingers find his asscrack is slick; taking advantage of the fact, I slide a fore-finger deep, making him buck in my mouth. A moan escapes my throat around him as Apollo starts fucking me with the dildo and eating me out.

Dr. Martins abruptly pulls out of my mouth, causing my finger to slip from him. Marcus is directing him, and I raise my head, watching myself in the monitor with a close up of me getting plundered and licked. *My pussy looks pretty good from this angle with the contrast of the gold. If I weren't the one starring in it, I could watch this porn.* The doctor climbs over me on all fours before resting back to give me an excellent view of his taint. Marcus tells me to stick out my tongue and keep it out while the whole kit and caboodle settles over my face. Bypassing his dick, the doctor lowers his ass to my mouth. I clamp my lips shut until I feel a sharp yank to my hair that makes me yelp and give in.

I tentatively probe his ass until the tip of my tongue slides a little into the tight ring, and I taste vanilla. I get it now, the lube is flavored, so I can eat his ass out. Not being as bad as I thought it would be, I grab his cheeks in my hands, spreading them, and tilt my chin back. I can see another monitor behind me with the guys under it now that I don't have balls blocking my view. They're completely nude and seem to be enjoying this if their hard dicks are any indication.

I flutter my tongue all over Dr. Martins' asshole before I start sucking and nibbling at the edges. I use my thumbs and slide them both in just enough to spear my tongue and mimic fucking him with it. Pressing in and burying it as deep as I can, I grab the ring of muscle with my teeth, biting down gently to hold in place. Wrapping my lips around it all, I suck. Hard. I alternate penetrating with my tongue and sucking with him impaled on it, and I feel his ass start to spasm against my lips. Watching his expression in the monitor, his face screws up like he's going to come. Before he does, he quickly climbs off me for Emmett to take his place.

Emmett climbs straight over my head, assuming the same position the doctor had, and I notice the plug is still in him. I suck on his balls as I work the plug out, hoping I don't accidentally pull the center out instead, garnering a moan from him. While I do this, the doctor takes Apollo's position between my legs, pushes my knees back high, lines the head of his cock up, and plunges in, in one swift movement. I moan at the size of him. He's long and thick and fills me up. I'm worked open from all the previous action, so there is no resistance to his entry.

He starts a fast pace, pounding in and out while I turn my attention back to Emmett, and as he's been loosened from the plug, I spread him wide and spear deep with my tongue. He too tastes of vanilla. I clamp his ring with my teeth and start sucking. Fucking him with my tongue is easier with him stretched than it was with the doctor, and I can do a better job of it. He's soon panting and flexing in my mouth when Dr. Martins shoves deep and starts pulsing with his own orgasm.

Emmett climbs off at some unseen signal, and as the doctor pulls out, the camera picks up the cum running out of me and down my crack. I'm annoyed and horny as hell now, after not getting off from the doctor. In this case, at least there's several more to go. *Hopefully,* one *of them can manage to do the job.* I give the doctor a side-eyed glare in case he's unaware how under-whelming his performance was.

Emmett takes his turn between my legs as I keep watch on the monitor. Marcus moves up behind him while Emmett enters me slower than the doctor had, a grimace wrinkling up his angelic features. In the monitor I see myself stretched wide around him with the plug end poking out and the clamp shining under the spotlight. Marcus wields a large black sili-cone dildo, probing Emmett's ass. He plants it deep as Emmett begins moving in me. Marcus is just holding steady pressure, so as Emmett fucks me, on every backstroke, he impales himself to the hilt.

I watch in the monitor between his legs as Rex settles over me, tilting my head back to fuck my mouth. Emmett tenses preceding his orgasm, and Marcus pulls him out of me, signaling Rex to take Emmett into his mouth to choke him down balls deep while Marcus impales his ass until he comes with a yell into Rex's mouth. Rex blanches at the cum in his mouth but swallows at Marcus' glare, gagging a little as he does.

Emmett is sweaty and done, having gone limp, but I see Marcus bind the dildo up in him tightly through a ring on the back anyway. Rebinding his wrists behind his back, he's placed over a standing wedge type thing with his ass in the air for all to see his hole stretched around the silicone intrusion.

I pop Rex's plug loose while Apollo gets into position between my thighs. None of these men are small, and I *still* haven't gotten off. I'm getting pissed at their selfishness and the spectacle being made of me. He starts a rhythm that *might* make me come soon, and I notice that even his dick is the same dusky color as his skin. And he's bare as well, all the baby birds in here are wigging me out.

I pull Rex's hole to my mouth, hoping the sooner this is

done the sooner I can shower and go to bed. I go to town on his ass, and soon I have him groaning and climbing off; apparently no one is supposed to come in my mouth. I see Marcus in the monitor guiding him behind Apollo, who has his pants around his ankles and his shirt unbuttoned. I'm surprised to see a tube go in Apollo as Rex holds his cheeks out for Marcus. Marcus puts a condom on Rex, and Apollo leans over me more. I can't figure out the method for wearing protection or not, and it's really starting to concern me. Ignoring it for the moment as there's nothing I can do, I assist Rex by reaching out to hold Apollo open for him. *Fair's fair, after earlier.*

Rex pushes two fingers deep, working in and out before placing the head of his dick on Apollo's hole, then pressing in. Apollo grunts and wiggles back, but otherwise doesn't react to being fucked. I'd guess it's a usual occurrence for him. Rex pushes him down further over me, grabs his hips and works back and forth in short bursts until he's sinking his entire length in. Marcus leaves them and drops his pants, revealing his lack of underwear. His dick is hard and an average length, but it's wide. I mean, *very* wide. He points it down and presses it to my lips. I dart my tongue out and lick the tip, not certain I can get my mouth around it without getting him with my teeth. He gets impatient and tilts my head back, pressing my lower jaw down with his thumb. *I'll just let him handle it, then. If he gets scraped, it's on him.*

I open wide, and the tip gets partially in when he stops and taps my chin again. I open as far as I can, feeling too strained at the hinge in my mouth. He carefully guides himself in until he hits the back of my throat. *That ain't fitting, buddy boy.* He holds there, rocking forward, but I can't get my esophagus to relax, and he's blocking all my air. I tap the side of his leg, and thankfully, he pulls back long enough for me to take a breath. With Apollo still riding me and Rex behind him, I get distracted and inadvertently relax enough that when Marcus goes back in and gets to my throat, he keeps going until he's seated fully. I startle at the burn of it, and my throat convulses around him causing him to flex his hips forward. I tap him again to remind him I can't breathe like this. He starts moving in and out to the same rhythm Apollo is. I can only hope he doesn't last long.

I briefly close my eyes, then open them again when Marcus puts one knee next to my head to lean further over my face for a better angle. Glancing between his legs, I meet Braeden's eyes. He's in the process of kneeling behind Marcus, and I'm thinking he's up to something besides what he's been instructed.

Without preamble, he leans in and takes both testicles into mouth. *Now that's talent.* Marcus growls in his throat, still working in and out but losing his stride with the tug on his balls. I wink at my bestie, realizing Marcus can't choke me on his dick unless he wants to hurt himself. Brade has one of the tubes of lubricant in his hand, and I'm really wondering what he has planned.

I start sucking, and instantly draw Marcus' attention from the man behind him. Braeden licks a line up to his ass, taking his time around the rim and probing him with his thick tongue. Using one hand to hold him open, he licks and sucks, causing Marcus to pause his movement for a moment. When he picks his pace back up, I watch as Brade moves the tube up into position. I attempt to go porn star on him, moaning in my throat and hoping the vibrations will distract him. An instant later, the tube breaches him. He starts to pull back with surprise, but it's already been emptied and removed, and Braeden is slipping his fingers into him now, pumping in and out rapidly. The suddenness has Marcus groaning in what sounds like pleasure, and he surges back into my throat.

From between my legs, Apollo lifts my feet up for Marcus to hold then pull back far enough that my knees rest near my ears. The new angle is doing it for me, and when Apollo starts flicking the clamp on my clit, I come undone, my pussy locking down on Apollo's dick. He stays buried to the hilt while Rex takes over and rides them both to completion. Marcus withdraws and signals Braeden to release him as well.

In the monitor overhead is a close up of Rex slipping from Apollo, trailing his spunk with him. *Almost done.* I'm beyond exhausted and really want to sleep now. My legs are released to relax down, and Apollo is rebinding Rex and placing him over another wedge next to Emmett. As Marcus gets in place to take his turn between my legs and Braeden steps up to my head, I watch the monitor as Rex gets a new plug installed and bound into him. They're all still taking this without obvious complaint, and it's making me batty. *Is insta-brainwash a thing?*

Marcus hitches my feet over his shoulders as Apollo comes up next to us. He gestures for Braeden to get on with it. I glance at him, and he winks at me. *Fuck, I love my bestie for his support no matter the situation. My total ride or die bitch.*

Opening my mouth, I tilt my chin, and he slides all the way home. *I should have asked him for tips on fellatio years ago.* He'd covered himself with some of that vanilla stuff when I wasn't paying attention. It leaves a greasy coating in my mouth but makes it easier to take him. I bet that's what the wink was for. Apollo reaches over to add more of the shit to the outside of my swollen pussy. As Marcus starts pushing the head of his cock in, I'm grateful for the extra. *Jizz isn't comparable to heavy duty lube.* The man is *seriously* wide.

As used as my snatch has already been tonight, it's still not sloppy enough to take him without effort. He gets past the tip, causing the ring of my opening to burn as it's stretched to its limit, the steady pushing results in a sensation much like what I imagine taking a soda can in the crotch would feel like. I'm moaning around Braeden, and not in a good way. As I glance at the monitor, I can see he's only halfway in, but I don't know how much more I can handle in one go. Anticipating my urge to balk, Apollo reaches for one of the nipple clamps, releasing it. My scream is muffled with the dick in my throat, and Apollo brings Braeden's hand up to start rubbing the abused tip. Seconds later, the other is released, and I scream again. Brade doesn't need prompting to reach his hand out to soothe it.

During all this, Marcus shoves his way home. My nipples and my pussy are on pure fire, and Braeden keeps plunging in and out of my throat. Marcus starts with punishing thrusts that gradually begin to move toward pleasurable instead of the burn from before. Above me, Braeden grunts, and I see Apollo is behind him removing his plug. He pulls out of my mouth and climbs over me so I can eat his ass. *These people need a new pastime, and I need some industrial fucking Listerine.* Apollo, now that he's no longer busy with the others, holds Braeden's ass open and guides him down to my mouth. I do my best with my tired tongue and lips, nearly bringing him to completion in a few short moments.

Apollo removes him as his legs begin to tremble and Marcus barks out a curse with his own orgasm. I'm flooded with more fluid. None have worn condoms, which I'll be addressing the instant it's feasible, or cleaned me up, and I have alternated between being fucked dry and being a sopping mess. Tilted as I am on the wedge, it has to run over or been pushed out each time a dick enters me. I know when I stand up, it's going to be gross.

Braeden is led around, and my legs are pulled up and out on either side by Marcus and Apollo. My bestie traces his fingers over my sore mound briefly before meeting my tired gaze. I keep eye contact as he enters me. Even after Marcus, I've maintained some elasticity. *Gonna have to do some exercises or get loose in this crowd.* Braeden is close to Marcus' girth, but not quite there. He's several inches longer though and soon hits my cervix. I involuntarily flinch away a little. It's been well abused already and is extra sensitive by this point.

He tries to back up, but Marcus shakes his head at him. Clearing the expression from his face and pushing until his balls are against my ass, he makes me squirm and grimace at the sharp prick of pain. Even at his lazy rolling pace, boy has moves that get my attention even through the discomfort. With a hip tilt and rotation, he's hitting all my spots with every stroke. I help as much as I can from my position, which isn't much, but I feel myself building to a climax. Soon, I'm straining towards it. *Never thought my best friend could rock my world so well.*

Apollo reaches down, I think, to flick the clamp on my clit. Instead, he releases it, allowing the blood to rush back into it, causing a pleasure/pain so intense I let out a guttural cry and instantly come around Braeden, dragging at his dick as he tries to keep moving. He can't keep it up and comes with a quiet moan. We rest that way for a moment before Marcus removes Braeden and binds him, taking him over to another wedge prop. He drapes his tall frame over it and mounts another large plug in him, tying it up like the others.

Apollo removes the pillow, and when I sit up, as I suspect, the fluids that were released into me slip out. Apollo hands me several wet wipes, and I clean up as well as I can, but I think I just succeed more in pushing it around than anything else but oh well.

The lights on the platform dim, forcing me to face what I've blocked out the entire time.

People watching— hungry people watching. I want to hide from those expressions. They want one or more of us, to use us like this constantly. I cringe, imagining that sort of life.

12

DO OR DIE

Marcus and the doctor help my three guys up, and Apollo lines us up as he takes a bow. *Fuck that.* Some clap in appreciation, while others inquire about prices. After Apollo tells them that we already have a prospective buyer and that none of them may purchase us at this time, one man speaks up.

"The only one I saw with your mark was your companion, Marcus. Therefore, they *are* available for purchase." Apollo and Marcus both curse under their breath. I don't really understand what's happening, but the vibe coming off Apollo and Marcus is worrisome. Pausing for a moment, I do recall a raised sun mark on the inside of Marcus' thigh when he was over me. I didn't think much of it at the time since I was otherwise occupied, but now that I am, I realize that it's a brand. Like on cattle. Like burned into the skin. Like permanently marked. *Oh, fuck no. No one is branding me.* They're going to have a massive fight on their hands if they try.

"Their marks will be completed as soon as their training is over. They take months to fully heal— I don't need a delay if it gets infected," he states coldly to the man. I think that's going to be the end of it; then Mr. Vitti speaks up.

"There's time before they need to be presented again. They can have a few days to heal up, so I don't see the point in a delay. It's best to mark the pets sooner rather than later." *What a piece of camel crap.* "I just also happen to have the iron that was used for Marcus." Concluding his bullshit Mr. Vitti pulls out a torch pen with a metal sun that has little wavy rays extending from it. It's attached a few inches above the tip of the small burner, with the medallion itself being about the size of a quarter.

I feel the color drain from my face so fast I get light-headed and look to Braeden in a panic. He appears stoic, but I know he's just as freaked out as I am. Glancing over to Rex and Emmett, the former looking pissed, while the latter is nearly green, I have the short-lived thought of wondering if we can fight our way out. Unfortunately, we're underground in an unknown location with who knows how many guards. Not to mention the guys all have their hands bound behind them with things up their asses that are going to make running difficult. Begrudgingly, I wait for Apollo to get us out of this.

"I don't agree with this. They are mine to train as I see fit." Mr. Vitti smiles, and it's disturbing to say the least. I don't think Apollo is going to win this one, and I start to feel short of breath. The man is straight evil. *If he brands me, I'll find a way to kill him.* Something of my thoughts must have shown on my face as he loses his smile.

"This is my operation, and I desire the pets be branded." He snaps his fingers, and instantaneously, we all have guards surrounding us. "We'll start with *her*." He gestures to me, and the guys start to struggle, mostly ineffectively.

He only put one guard on me, and I immediately lash out at him. Bringing my elbow back, I smash it up into his nose. He instantly drops me, groaning with blood pouring between his fingers. Another guard comes up and backhands me, and I barely keep my feet. I taste blood in my mouth, and I spit it out at the feet of the man that hit me in a show of defiance, maintaining the sneer on my face despite the discomfort.

The guys are all struggling in earnest, and another man comes up with a bottle of capsules in his hand. He tries forcing the first one into Rex's mouth, but between the other guard's difficulty to hold on to him and the movement of his head, it quickly becomes apparent that this tactic isn't going to work. The man gives up and goes to a cupboard, returning with a box full of syringes that are topped with thin short tubing instead of needles. Apollo has gone to step up to stop him when his father gives him a look I can't interpret, halting Apollo in his tracks.

"All of you cease struggling now, or Four will receive the punishment for all of you." This comes from Marcus, and the others turn to glare at him in anger and disbelief, but obey nonetheless. None of them want me hurt. I go to speak, and when I open my mouth to tell them not to stop on my account, something slips over my face and through my teeth so quickly and unexpectedly I don't even have a chance to close my mouth. It's a gag tasting of leather, holding my mouth open as if I were a horse with a bit. I can still make some noise, but nothing intelligible comes out. The buckle is fastened behind my head, and my hands are cuffed in padded velcro bracelets behind my back.

The man with the syringes moves back to Rex, and the guards bend him over, exposing his stuffed ass. The man slides the tubing in next to the dildo and empties the contents into him, following with both Emmett and Braeden. On his way past the doctor, he nods his head, and two guards grab him bending him over as well. Apollo is arguing that the doctor isn't a trainee, and his father states that as part of his training team he belongs to him just as Marcus does.

"Brent is your *nephew*, you insisted he be brought in as part of the family business for continued support for his mom and sister. He's not part of this, he's paying off his school loans and providing for his family." Apollo is earnest and slightly panicked, while Brent is resigned.

I don't know what kind of fucked up family dynamic this is, but Apollo isn't having any effect on his father.

"He's not listed as a trainer as you are. As such, he's part of the trainee program. Enough of this unless you're admitting you can't handle the duties of being my heir." That doesn't sound good, and from the strain on Apollo's face it's a very definite threat

Robert waves his hand at Apollo's silence and the doctor receives the same treatment as the others. As he comes toward me, I see the guys' eyes going slightly vacant, and Marcus reaches out a hand to trail over Emmett's chest, eliciting a moan from him.

"How much did you give them?" Apollo asks. "You know they can overdose on that shit on top of what they've already been given since arriving here!" *Wait, what?! They're drugging us?* As the man goes for the flesh between my legs, I kick out, and the syringe flies out of his hand. The man is furious, but answers Apollo as he goes back to his cupboard of drugs.

"It's a short-term dose. They'll remember mostly everything, and it will amplify feeling, yet it will keep them blissed out long enough to get this done." *Amplify feeling? Oh, fuck no! A branding. Amplified. Fuck that shit.*

"You're seriously going to *increase* the pain of being *branded*?" Apollo asks incredulously. Obviously, I'm not the only one that has a major fucking problem with it. At least it's one small step to trusting him, which I'd enjoy, except ya know, the whole trying to brand me fuckery. *Well maybe not, he* is *drugging my ass.* I'm still angry about it, but it's not the appropriate time to deal with that issue either.

The man comes back, and two more guards have appeared in front of me— one to take each leg and spread them. The man wielding the syringe seems to go for my vagina to put in the tubing, but instead spreads my lips wide and taut, using his body to hide what he's actually doing as he pushes into my urethra and quickly depresses the plunger. The liquid shoots up into my bladder, burning a path of pure acid.

I shriek behind the gag, and Apollo is instantly at my side to investigate what's wrong. He sees the man pull the tubing out with a trickle of urine with it that I couldn't control coming out, it hurts so badly. I'm embarrassed and in pain.

"What the fuck, Robert? Your man is damaging my property!" Get the hell away from her!" Apollo is pissed, but the damage is already done.

The man mutters 'oops', but I see his smirk. I'll do him some serious damage if I ever get my hands on him alone. Apollo kneels down to check me out. All the guys are staring, but can't really seem to concentrate. *That doctor would come in real handy about now.*

Apollo echoes my thoughts. "These are the types of things I need Brent for, and now he's doped up and useless to me. Marcus, come help me." I'm wondering how bad it is as Marcus comes up with a wet wipe and a basin.

"Four, I need you to empty your bladder. That stuff isn't meant to be in there, and I don't know what a dose that size will do to you." *I have to piss into a bucket that Marcus is holding while being held by four strange men, and everyone is just standing and sitting here watching.* I want to cry, but I won't do it in front of these people. I close my eyes and try to relax. The burning is instantaneous, and I cry out, immediately stopping the flow of urine. My poor urethra was torn, I know it. It's throbbing like I smashed it with a hammer.

Quieter this time, Marcus gives me a look of sympathy. "I know it burns like a bitch. Power through it, and I'll clean you up and check the damage." I can feel some of the drug taking effect, and that prompts me to hurry. It burns the entire time, and I do my best to hold back the noises of pain, not wanting to give the asshole that did this the satisfaction.

Shortly, I'm done, allowing Marcus to clean me up and examine the area. "There's some blood in her urine, and the edges look a little torn, but I think she'll be okay with some antibiotics to prevent infection and a few days' rest. That tubing wasn't even sterile; he screwed it on with his bare hands." Marcus is addressing Apollo in a low menacing voice. Apollo, in turn, addresses his father.

"Due to the injury— and possible infection— resulting from the unsanitary use of that syringe, my trainee will need a week's worth of antibiotics. During that time I will have her refrain from training. The other issues will cause several days for all of them to be at rest. I will do light training with the others after the marks have healed enough to allow ease of movement, but nothing involved until I have them all back together. I don't want to repeat instructions individually due to this incompetence." Mr. Vitti looks annoyed but nods his head at Apollo's demands. Turning to me, he continues quietly, "I'm sorry, but we can't chance giving you anything else right now to help. As soon as Brent recovers, I'll have him look you over and find out what we can give you. I'm afraid this is going to be rather unpleasant without aid."

With that, he steps over to his father to take the brand. On his way back he makes the mistake of making eye contact with me. He seems to understand that this is the breaking point and his life may be in just as much danger as mine is currently in. I hear a click, and the torch lights, heating up the metal above it. I begin to struggle again, but Marcus comes in and slaps the insides of my spread thighs. I squeal, and he does it again and again, alternating between the two. The skin becomes red and welted and is beginning to lose feeling. He applies a cold gel on the skin of my left inner thigh. *Right where his brand was,* I remember in a panic. When Marcus reaches out with both hands and makes a circle high up on my inner thigh and holds the skin firmly in place, I notice the sensation of his touch is dulled and realize the gel must have been some sort of numbing agent. I start up struggling again anyway as Apollo comes toward me with a blank expression on his face. A guard holds a gun up to Braeden's head, and I freeze, ceasing all resistance.

I slump in defeat for a moment, but my anxiety is through the roof at the hot brand coming toward me, and I start to tremble, unable to stop. Apollo has my leg brought as far away from the rest of my body as possible and lines up the hot metal. I can feel the heat radiating off it while it's still several inches away. Apollo tells me to hold as still as possible so that it doesn't skip or burn too deeply. I look at the guys, and they're still mostly lethargic, but when I look to Marcus, I actually see compassion. I guess he would have some since he had to go through this already.

I close my eyes, as I don't want to see it happen, when Apollo presses something, causing the torch to go out. Swiftly, he presses the hot metal to my skin, hard, and I scream at the pain. Time stands still as he seems to hold it there for what feels like forever but was probably only mere seconds. The stench of my own seared flesh and the feeling of skin pulling with the metal as he removes it makes my stomach roll.

I attempt to hold the vomit down, but it's no use, and I throw up with the gag still in my mouth. I temporarily forget the pain in my leg as I choke on my own puke. Marcus, acting quickly, gets the gag off me and starts wiping me up, muttering curses under his breath. Thankfully, it was mostly liquid as we hadn't exactly gotten to eat much since we've been here. After he gets me cleaned up, he puts an ointment and a large cushion type bandage over the raw skin. Afraid to look, I glance away.

The only even remotely good thing is that my bladder was already empty, or I may have pissed myself as well.

Marcus leaves me to assist Apollo with the others, and they all get the same routine minus the thigh slapping while I hang there in the guards' grips. At least it's simpler since they're drugged, but they still scream. Not as loud as mine was, and they're not as active as a sober person would be, needing only one other guard to hold them. Marcus bandages them all, and the guards that held them lead them all back to the room. The guards had tried to set me on my feet, but between the pain of my leg and my pee hole, and the drugs having a bad effect after all, I can't stand very well. Marcus scoops me up in his arms and carries me back down to the room with Apollo opening doors for him as we go.

13

ROLLING ON MOLLY

After we arrive back in the room, we find Brent trying to undo the bindings on Rex and failing miserably. He keeps fumbling the ties or Rex moans and moves. Marcus gently sets me down on the couch, and he and Apollo move to help. Apollo sends Brent over to sit by me, and we both watch as they're unbound. Rex grabs— and starts stroking — himself as soon as his hands are free. Apollo reaches out to stop him.

"Marcus let's get them all in the bathroom and into the shower. We all need to bathe, and all the guys are probably going to be like this. I'm not sure why Brent isn't too." Marcus grabs Emmett and Braeden, and as out of it as he is, Brade comes back to me instead of following. I take his arm and let him lead with me limping along. At least I can walk on my own two feet now. I register what Apollo said about Brent and remember I'm livid with Apollo and Marcus.

"Wouldn't have anything to do with the fact that you've been regularly dosing us, would it? And that Brent just got a first dose?" Marcus just looks at me and doesn't say anything. I take that as a yes. I'll deal with them later, *after* we've all cleaned up and slept.

Marcus already has the huge bath going and is rinsing Rex off in the shower while Rex is jacking himself off. All those muscles are flexing and straining towards his release. He doesn't even act like his leg hurts. His bandage doesn't seem to be getting wet though, the water running over and off it. The thin adhesive plastic membrane must be waterproof. Marcus gets him to widen his legs and bend forward so he can remove the plug from his ass. When he pulls it out, Rex moans with his head back and eyes closed. He tries to rub back against the plug, but it's gone. Apollo seems exasperated.

"Marcus, just help him get off and then get him in the tub. It's our own fault he's in this shape." Marcus, taking the suggestion, spreads Rex's cheeks back open and easily slips the plug back in getting a moan from Rex as his hand speeds up. Marcus begins fucking Rex in the ass with the plug, one hand holding his cheek to the side, while the other pops the plug in and out rapidly. Marcus must sense it isn't enough, or he's impatient, and pushes in past the wide base of the plug with his fingers still wrapped around it to grind it into him, eliciting a yell from Rex. He starts spurting from his engorged dick, and Marcus pulls out against his clenching ass before placing the plug on a shelf to finish rinsing Rex then guiding him into the now filled tub of tepid water.

I do hear one of them mumble about the temperature, so I'm guessing the burn is beginning to register. Apollo puts Brent in and quickly rinses him then puts him in the tub with Rex. Emmett is next with Apollo joining him, and he's almost as bad as Rex. Rubbing his ass on Apollo as he removes the dildo. Apollo doesn't even try to stop him, just gets down on his knees and starts sucking Emmett off. He puts one of Emmett's legs over his shoulders and enters him with the dildo, fucking him hard and deep with it in time to the sucking.

Emmett's dick disappears down Apollo's throat in tandem with the dildo disappearing in his ass. Apollo can suck a dick like a pro. He's taking it all the way to the base and appears to be swallowing around it until he has to come up for air. One last hold and Emmett takes a hand off the shower wall to palm the back of Apollo's head, giving a few unsteady jerks in and out, then pressing against his face tight. Apollo continues to fuck him with the dildo until he's completely done before removing it.

Marcus comes over to help me and Braeden as Apollo leads Emmett away to babysit all three now in the tub. Marcus carefully removes the small faux plug from me, and I rinse off. I help him rinse Braeden, and he removes his plug while I help support him. He moans and rubs against me some, but pushes Marcus away when he goes to assist him.

"I'm fine. Just feel like I'm on a shit ton of ecstasy right now. I can feel and understand everything, but it's like trying to wade through mud to get anything done intentionally."

"You should never have gotten that large of a dose, even if you hadn't already had some. It's dangerous." Marcus is pissed, but thankfully not at us.

"Little bird? You alright? I'm sorry I couldn't help you." His words are slightly slurred as he puts his arms around me and holds me tight against him. He whispers in my ear, "I'll kill them all for hurting you." If Marcus hears, he doesn't let on, or maybe he agrees with him. "Let's get you in the tub. Marcus, can you help her in? I can handle myself, but I'm not steady enough yet to be picking her up." Marcus nods and swings me up in his arms again, settling us both into the tub. As soon as Braeden is in, he pulls me onto his lap. "Let me check, okay?" I shake my head no. I don't want him touching it. Not only because it hurts, but because it's embarrassing, and I'll keep what dignity I have left wherever I can. "Okay, baby bird, but the doctor will be checking as soon as he's coherent." There's a tone that I don't dare refuse coming from my best friend, so I keep quiet and snuggle up to him in the warm water and drift off.

I wake up to a quiet argument. Rex is furious with Apollo. I decide to stay quiet and listen, but I'm sure Braeden knows I'm awake.

"You let them get branded! Like cattle! What the fuck, Apollo?" Was he not upset about him and Emmett? Maybe they had been warned it was a possibility?

"I didn't have much of a choice. Robert isn't a normal father — or person for that matter. If he even had a *thought* I was betraying him, he would execute us all. I'm sorry, I did what I could to stop it. He even included Brent, and that was never supposed to happen either."

"What about the drugs? Emmett and I discounted feeling off as an environmental effect. Of course, Lark is the only one that kept voicing her concerns that something was off, mumbling about that kidnapper's syndrome. She's better at fighting it, too, apparently." At least Rex had noticed I'd been complaining.

"She does seem to have some natural resistance to it." Dr. Martins' voice interrupts the conversation— guess his has worn off too.

"Robert demands random blood and urine tests. If you don't have any traces in your system, he will know something is up. He at least saw firsthand that Lark isn't very affected by it. That could also be a bad thing as he could decide she needs something stronger." Apollo's words leave a moment of tense silence.

"One thing that hasn't been addressed is if she's going to be punished." I stiffen at Marcus' statement, and Braeden tightens his arms around me.

"Why would she be punished?" Braeden is pissed, and Marcus answers him.

"She fucked up the guards pretty good, and she did it all in front of Robert. He won't let that slide without retribution."

"That bastard assistant of his got his revenge already." Braeden is adamant, but I don't think it's going to be enough. My fears are confirmed when Apollo confirms it.

"He'll want a public punishment to demonstrate what happens to anyone who defies him. I'll negotiate to be the one to decide the punishment, but I'll tell you now— it will have to be something suitable and harsh enough to appease him. I should be able to get him to agree to nothing that will leave scars, so as not to drive the selling price down." I hate being talked about like an animal at an auction. Marcus speaks up before Braeden can get anything coherent out of his mouth.

"I'll be the one to administer it, so there won't be a chance of one of his guards doing any more damage."

"Can we just leave it for later? Apollo, I'm sure you'll do your best, and as we're still stuck here, I don't see any way of getting out of it. I just want to get clean and dressed and sleep." Ending on a snap, I start to wash with pruned fingers, but Braeden takes over, and I see the other guys watching surreptitiously as they clean up themselves. The water is tinged with the gold dust by the time he's finished with me. Marcus helps Braeden get me out, and they get all of us dried off and dressed. Moving back into the bedroom, I see what I was too out of it to notice earlier. There is one huge bed in the room now. It looks like two king-sized mattresses have been hooked together. I turn to ask about it, but Marcus beats me to it.

"It's safer to all sleep in one bed. It will be harder for someone to grab one of you without the others noticing. We used 'training' as an excuse, but the single beds could potentially let someone get grabbed, and you wouldn't notice until it's too late. There's a panic button on the headboard that alerts both me and Apollo and another under the kitchen counter if someone tries to do anything without one of us here. We'll also give you the code to the training room as it can double as a safe room unless someone has the override code. As far as I know only Apollo and Robert have those." I see the upside of the bed, but the downside is I'm going to be sleeping with all these men, most of whom I don't want near me. Good thing I'm too hurt and exhausted to get too worked up about it.

Marcus and Braeden crawl up with me in between them on one side. Although I'm a little surprised that Marcus is staying, I don't question it. We seem to have bonded some in the last couple hours or so. I'm not sure why I don't find him so intimidating anymore, but I don't. I cuddle my front into Braeden with my head on his chest and Marcus spoons up behind me with an arm slung over us both. I barely register the others getting into bed before I'm out.

14

A P.I.T.A. (PAIN IN THE ASS)

I wake up to voices, again. I sit up gingerly due to the pain in my leg and crotch, trying to hear what's going on. I notice I'm alone in the huge bed. Apollo is arguing with someone, then Marcus comes into the room.

"How long have I been asleep? Where is everyone else at?" Marcus helps me stand— I'm disoriented from sleep and need to pee, but otherwise feel much better.

"You've been out for sixteen hours." I can't believe I slept that long. I make it to the bathroom, and Marcus doesn't move from the doorway when I try to close it. "I think you can piss in front of me after everything. I need to tell you what's happening as soon as possible before you leave this room. Apollo can only stall for so long." My punishment. Should have known it would be sooner rather than later. I give up on the door and sit down to do my business, not looking at Marcus. I expect it to burn, but it isn't as bad as I'd thought it would be. I guess all the sleep let me heal up some. "The others will stay with the doctor in the training room, and it will just be me, you, and Apollo."

"What's my punishment?" I don't really care. I actually feel slightly detached. I don't want to be present in this nightmare anymore. Being in this suite and training room are bad enough, but dealing with the sick perverts that enjoy the pain and degradation of human beings disgusts me. Marcus must be able to tell I'm on the edge of checking out.

"Hey now, none of that. Stay with me here. We'll get you out of here as soon as we can. If they aren't all rounded up and brought down together, none of us will ever be safe." I hadn't thought of that aspect. I just wanted to know why no one had come to get us yet. "I'd rather not tell you. It's not horrible, but I just want to keep you calm. And no worries on the drugs— there won't be any lubricant. Clean up and put your hair in a bun on top of your head. I'll leave a robe on the bed, and you won't need anything else." *Of course, I'll be naked, what's new?*

I nod my head, seeing no point in fighting it. "I'll be right out." I clean up and prepare as instructed. I'm nervous and want to know what's going to happen, but at the same time I don't want to know. All I can do is trust that Apollo managed to intervene on my behalf. I find it strange that I trust him enough to believe that neither he, nor Marcus, would deliberately hurt me— not if they could avoid it, anyway. I suppose it's something to do with knowing what they're trying to accomplish and the fact that they really haven't hurt me, well, besides the whole drugging thing. Completely fucked up in their sexual activities, but I'm not sure how normal I would have been in the same environment all my life. I come out to find Apollo and Marcus waiting on me. Marcus indicates some slippers on the floor, and I slide them on. Apollo puts his arm around me and raises one hand to tip my face up to his using my chin.

"Marcus will be performing the punishment, and I will supervise. Be prepared for someone to request for you to be fucked afterwards. If that happens— I will do it. No one else will touch you. Before we leave, I want to change your bandage and check the mark for infection."

Marcus peels the adhesive off, and I have to hold in a squeal. *That shit hurts!* After he gets it off, he spritzes it with some disinfectant and blots it. Applying a fresh layer of salve, he covers it with a new clean bandage. "It looks pretty good, actually. How is the pain level?"

"It's really sore, but as long as I don't touch or move it too much it's tolerable." Apollo nods, as if he expected as much, and opens the door. I follow him down the hallway while Marcus brings up the rear. I almost snicker at that thought. *Bringing up the rear. That's so appropriate here.*

WE GET BACK to the same room with the dais, and there aren't as many people as last time, but enough to make me even more nervous about what will be happening. The guard with the broken nose is there glaring at me, as well. Robert is waiting and makes his announcement as Apollo takes up position at the base of the dais and Marcus leads me up on it.

"My son has brought his training slave for her punishment. A pound of flesh is what I requested. Instead, I've agreed to give her a pound of flesh instead."

I don't understand what he's talking about, but as I'm being led towards a bench that is going to put my ass and pussy on display as soon as I bend over it, I'm slightly distracted. I cooperate with Marcus— disrobing— before leaning over it. He gets me into position and secures my hands at the small of my back. My feet and knees are placed in holds made for them, and I'm squatting like a frog tipped upside down, completely exposed. A strap comes over my back, threaded under my arms and holds me down to the bench. More come around to bind my legs into position.

Robert continues after I'm secured, and the close-up monitors come on. One is directly in my line of sight. *I don't doubt was done on purpose.* "A pound of ginger flesh, a figging she won't soon forget." *What the fuck is figging, and what are they doing with ginger?* I watch as Marcus pulls out a monster ginger root that resembles a hand. As I'm wondering what he thinks he's going to do with that I see him take a knife and cut out a finger-like stem through the meaty part of the root. It's at least as long as his hand and several fingers worth in diameter if not a little more.

I didn't even know ginger looked like that. Marcus begins peeling it and every so often dipping it in a bowl of ice water. Soon, he has a phallus shape that hasn't lost any of its size with a notch about a half inch from the base like the dildo plugs. I have a feeling I know where that's going. And Marcus said no lube. He places it in the bowl of water with the ice in it and moves on to another piece. This one he makes into two small flat discs, and after he rinses them, he gets behind me. Using a clamp with flat plates and a screw-type tightener, he pulls my clit down, stretching it until it burns, and I make a small noise of complaint. He tightens the clamp down, and before it's as tight as it goes, he slides those wet pieces of ginger on either side and another I didn't notice before, almost a tiny ball up, under the hood of my clit. He tightens it all down until it's secure and leaves it to hang. Two clips from it attach to my outer pussy lips to help keep it in place.

I don't notice anything right away, but Marcus grabbing a flexible paddle looking thing gets my attention quick. The first blow gets a surprised squeal from me. It stings and makes a loud cracking noise, but it doesn't hurt too bad. He continues on, alternating from cheek to cheek and each slap gets progressively more painful. On top of that I'm feeling a burning on my clit and can't wiggle away from it. I'm bracing for another blow when the slap comes between my legs, directly against the opening of my cunt. I see Marcus lick the paddle and realize I'm wet and turned on, and I'm silently crying. I don't know if it's a kink I never knew about, the ginger, or both, but this is *not* the place I should be finding out. My ass is on fire, and the fact that I'm wet seems to spur him on.

I can see out of my peripheral vision the rapt gazes of the audience, and I want to die of shame that they can see me in such a state. I don't actually care about Apollo and Marcus. As I discovered earlier, I'm comfortable enough with them now. Marcus comes up and holds my hole wide, glistening pink in the light above the clamped and obscenely stretched flesh, as he slides two fingers in, twisting them around to gather my juices. He walks to Apollo to offers them up. Apollo accepts and leans in, sucking the fingers clean, causing me to break out in a full body flush that they'd do something so vulgar.

At least the audience can't take their eyes off the show, and it's giving me a reprieve from feeling their attention. Marcus comes back and pulls the ginger rod from the bowl and my eyes widen when I see him headed for my ass instead of my pussy.

He quietly addresses me. "I can't use lube, or it will block the ginger from working." I'm not sure if it's true or not, but that's all the warning I receive before he places the freezing tip to my hole and starts to slide it up.

My clit is burning, and I dread what's about to happen in my ass. I screech at the forced intrusion, unable to hold it back. The water isn't doing anything to help it move inward, and my body strains to get away against the straps. He works it in, rocking and pushing until he gets it fully seated, and the ridge holds it in place. I don't notice anything at first, and Marcus resumes his paddling to my sobs. He's aiming at the backs of my thighs, avoiding my wound and my buttocks. I'm still twitching with the pain when the ginger starts to work.

As soon as he notices I'm wiggling more fervently, he begins massaging my butt, and I try to move in vain. Marcus pushes my cheeks together, crushing them around the root, and I scream at the intensity of the sensation, like my insides are on fire. He spreads them, and it's a small, short-lived relief until he presses them together again, pulling another yell from me. I don't know how long he alternates this way, but I'm crying loudly now, the haze of pain making everything unclear. And the audience, the sick fucks, are eating it up.

Finally, Marcus works the root out, and I hope it will stop burning soon. Before I can recover, I feel a wet finger going in my ass just barely inside, and I see Apollo with his condom covered dick out— his *dry* dick. Marcus smears a very small amount of lube on him, and I know it's not enough to take him in my sore ass comfortably. I'm trembling in dread and anticipation and breaking out in a nervous sweat on top of the burning I still have going on. I'm a mess.

Watching the monitor with trepidation, I can see the horrid clamp on my lips and clit that is still twitching with the burning sensation from the ginger. Meanwhile, the tip of Apollo's dick gets closer to my puckered hole. Marcus spreads my cheeks wide and puts his thumbs on either side of my rear opening— pulling outward and exposing the pink flesh inside — allowing Apollo to begin breaching me. He continues to push until he's made it past that tight ring and slides up into my rectum. The friction from the lack of lube makes me scream again, not to mention this being the first time I've ever been fucked in the ass. If I could move, I would hit him.

"Get off me! Fucker, *get off!*" I start spewing obscenities at him, and Robert gestures to one of his thugs. At the same time, Marcus comes up and tries to gag me with a rubber ball on a strap, but I thrash my head, avoiding him. Behind me, Apollo withdraws and then slams into me, making me stiffen and shriek, giving Marcus the opportunity to gag me. By the time I've recovered enough to stop crying, Marcus has the strap firmly secured. Apollo begins moving in and out rapidly, and I continue to scream behind the gag. Snot and tears are everywhere, and Marcus is fiddling with the clamps. As they begin to release and the blood rushes in, I briefly black out from the pain. When the darkness recedes, Apollo buries himself deep and pulses his release into my ass. Pulling out, the condom he wore is tinged with blood, and I know I'm not going to be sitting down comfortably any time soon. My hole is slow to close, and before it closes completely, Marcus rubs something that burns at first then numbs my opening before manipulating it shut. All the while, my face burns in embarrassment and rage.

The torso and leg straps are removed, but I can't stand once Marcus gets me upright— my legs are asleep. He wraps me in my robe and swings me up in his arms, turning to Apollo, who has at least tucked his dick back in his slacks, for permission leave. I'm still gagged with my hands bound behind me.

"Take her and clean her up. I'll be along shortly to discuss resuming training with Dr. Martins." Apollo moves to his father and begins speaking with him as Marcus carries me from the room. I glare at him, and his silver gaze meets my artic one.

"I'll remove them after you're out of danger." No apology, no sympathy, *nothing*. He obviously knows I'm going to attempt some damage as soon as I can. Once we get to the suite, he takes me straight to the bath and quickly removes my gag, seeming surprised as well as wary that I don't immediately start yelling at him. "Braeden and the others are in the training room with Brent, Apollo will let them know you're back," he explains as he unties my hands.

As I shake and rub them together the best I can, trying to get the feeling back into them, I'm glad Brade is busy. Besides me being embarrassed, I don't think his reaction would be a good thing.

15

R & R - RETRIBUTION AND REPRIEVE

A s soon as I can, I turn the shower on scalding, climb in on still tingling legs, and sit in the built-in seat as gingerly as possible. I detach one of the heads and let the water run over my belly, vagina, and across my ass. Marcus knocks, then opens the door, holding a glass of water and two red ibuprofen tablets. He takes in the scene as I reach, first for the pills, then the water. Eventually, he seems to get up the courage to speak.

"I'm sorry, Lark. It had to be believable, and if I hadn't gagged you, Robert would have sent one of his men to join in to silence you. Apollo will be hating himself for hurting you, but it got the punishment over with quickly in a manner that kept in line with what his father would expect." I nod and look away, ignoring him, and he eventually closes the door and leaves.

After a while I hear noises in the bathroom but can't muster the will to rouse myself to see who it is. Apollo appears, naked, in the shower with Marcus. He goes to pick me up, and I swing my fist and nail him straight in the balls, before grabbing what

I can between his legs, giving it a twist. He grabs himself and groans, hunched over.

"Fuck, Nightingale, I think you popped one," he hisses, checking out his parts. "Marcus said you weren't talking, should have known you were waiting on me." He's eventually able to straighten up and reaches for me again, warily this time. I let him, although I'm not sure I want him touching me. He settles back down with me in his lap and starts rubbing my hip. It feels good, so I don't complain. "I'm sorry I hurt you. I panicked when you started yelling and needed a distraction. It could have been so much worse than that. Will you let us make it up to you?" I'm not positive what they mean by make it up to me, but I can guess. I'll go along until I decide if I like it or not.

"Touch my ass and I'll castrate you both." Marcus holds up his hands, and Apollo says, 'of course not'.

He turns me so that my back is to his front, the water is running down my chest. He takes my legs and places them on either side of his and spreads them wide. Taking the shower-head, he turns on the massage setting and begins running it all over my front in hypnotic circles, while Marcus gets on his knees and buries his face in my crotch, licking and sucking gently above the showerhead.

As I warm up and respond to them, he adds his hands to the mix, exposing the underside of my clit to flick it back and forth with the tip of his tongue. It's still overly sensitive from the ginger, as if it got too much sun, but not quite burnt. Marcus' broad shoulders are directly in my view between my thighs. His upper body is extremely well defined, the movement of his arms flexing all those muscles, and I find myself tracing them without thinking about it. He slips a finger in me, testing my readiness. He adds another and begins stroking over the right spot inside.

Apollo puts the showerhead on a higher setting and settles it over my clit while Marcus continues to pump my pussy.

With his mouth free, he brings his head up to suck on a nipple. My head is lolling back on Apollo's shoulder, and soon I'm coming with a quiet moan. I try to close my legs as I finish, but Apollo spreads his knees further, keeping me open. Marcus adds another digit, moving more rapidly now. The other hand comes up to twist and pluck at the nipple not already in his mouth, soothing and igniting the burn all at once.

With an angle adjustment, Apollo has the water pulsing directly inside the hood of my clit eliciting a guttural grunting from my throat as I'm in sensation overload. The orgasm crashes over me, robbing me of sight from the spots dancing in my vision while I gasp and twitch with clenching muscles.

Apollo removes the showerhead, allowing me to relax marginally with Marcus still leaning down, licking and sucking and cleaning me up gently. I was already wrung out from the punishment, and now I can barely sit up by myself.

They get us all out of the shower and me into some comfortable, loose clothing. Marcus had wrapped my hair in a towel, and now he's gently rubbing the excess water out of it. Apollo brings a brush over nudging Marcus out of the way to detangle my hair for me. I can't help but feel slightly pampered at the treatment. If it wasn't for the situation and my sore ass and nether regions, I might even be able to relax and enjoy it. Finishing, Apollo scoops me up and carries me into the bedroom, climbing under the blankets that have already been turned down and snuggling my back into his chest with my head on his arm.

I don't mind the comfort he's offering— even if it feels somewhat odd. I figure comfort is comfort, and I'll take what I can get. Marcus comes in to cover us up and let us know he's going to check on the guys and let them know that we're back. Apparently they were in the training room working out. Glad that they'd kept busy, yet butthurt that they hadn't been here when I returned, I try to sleep.

I'm lightly dozing when I hear Braeden arguing with Marcus that he's going to check on me whether Marcus likes it or not. I blink my tired eyes open to find him crouched next to the bed in front of me.

"Hey, baby bird, how are you feeling? Do I need to fuck one of these guys up?" Marcus, of course, immediately gets his hackles up. Gray eyes flashing like lightning, he addresses Braeden.

"Try it, pretty boy." That's great, Brade hates being called pretty boy. Even if he is sinfully pretty, he could never be mistaken for anything other than masculine.

"I was talking to Lark, not you, Bondage Barbie. Lark, tell me you're alright, please." He must be really concerned since he's calling me Lark. I stretch a hand out to cup his bristly cheek.

"I'm fine, Brade. These two made sure I was safe. It wasn't as bad as it could have been. I'm just worn out right now. Can I take a nap without you killing anyone?" He covers my hand with his own and rubs his cheek against it, nodding his head and leaning in to kiss my forehead. As he's retreating, Apollo shows that he's been awake and listening.

"Where's mine? I'm tired too," he whines.

What a little petulant child trapped in this man's body. If he wasn't so spot on when needed, I'd be sure he was nutty as Grandma's almond brittle. And Grandma had loved her brittle. And almonds. Probably how she ended up in a diabetic coma when I was a kid. *Fuck, now I'm losing it. Like Grandma before she died.*

Brade just chuckles and leans over me, aiming for Apollo's forehead. Backing up with a 'hey', I have a feeling Apollo tipped his head and got one on the mouth instead. Braeden and Marcus step out and close the door behind them.

I think about Braeden not kissing on the mouth unless he's dating someone, he says it's too intimate. I guess that should have been a clue as well, as he never had a problem pecking me on the lips. We really need to get out of here and have a talk about this thing that's been exposed between us. This isn't the place to tell him I'd have reciprocated his feelings, had I known.

"You're a lucky girl, Lark Jones." I snort at that. *None* of this is 'lucky'. "That man is head over heels and so is that neanderthal in the other room. I wouldn't be surprised if his partner had some feelings as well, with the way I catch him looking at you." He snuggles me tighter as I refrain from answering. Surprisingly, I fall asleep and rest well for being in a possibly crazy criminal's arms.

WAKING UP, I'm hot and sweating and sandwiched between two large bodies. From the light filtering from the bathroom, I see Rex's relaxed features in front of me. My legs are entwined with his as they have been many times before. I feel a pang of sadness that we're no longer a couple, but I'm also still upset about how he handled the situation. If he was able to break it off so easily, then he couldn't have been as serious about our relationship as I was.

Turning my head to look isn't necessary to know that Braeden is the other body behind me. We've cuddled so frequently over the years that I recognize everything about him, sight or not. I try to figure out how to extricate myself without waking him up as my bladder is telling me to get to the toilet asap. I manage to slide out from between them and to the foot of the bed without disturbing them— noticing after I get up they've slid into the void I left and are almost snuggling each other. Emmett, Apollo, and Brent are in the bed as well, but Marcus is missing from the room.

I go to the bathroom and use the toilet, examining myself in the mirror while washing my hands. I find a pale face, with shadows under tawny eyes, and dark hair all a mess. I brush it out and replace the tie in it to keep it back and out of my face—not much else to do about the rest.

Stomach grumbling for food and wanting to see what time it is, I brush my teeth before heading out— stifling a giggle at Rex and Braeden as the former has tossed an arm and a leg over the latter. That's going to be a surprise to them both when they wake up.

Going out into the main area, I come upon Marcus on the couch watching an older movie that's one of my favorites. I catch Marcus' attention as I move into the kitchen area, and he pauses the show.

"Hungry, Lark?" I'm surprised, unsure he's ever called me by my name before.

"Umm...yeah. Just going to see what was in here. Do you want anything?" I rummage in the fridge and find Chinese in plastic containers. It smells good when I open a few and sniff them, so I start pulling them out and find a baking sheet in one of the cupboards to reheat it.

There's a little oven mounted in the wall of the kitchenette, and once I preheat it, I start arranging portions of orange and almond chicken, fried rice, lo mein, and stuffed wontons on the sheet. Finding plates, flatware, and napkins, I set them out on the little coffee table in front of the couch. I'm a little uncomfortable as Marcus is watching me move around and set everything up, but I'm determined not to let it bother me.

The oven finally dings, signaling that it's preheated, and I pop the pan in to let the food get hot while rummaging for drinks. There's root beer in the fridge, and, on a whim, I open the freezer and luck out with vanilla ice cream. Either they feed their slaves well, or Apollo or Marcus arranged for all of this. I'm going with the latter as I don't really see Apollo's father giving a crap about other human beings, besides basic care for his use.

After the food and floats are done, I take it all to the coffee table and am in the middle of filling my plate when I realize Marcus is still staring at me.

"What? Do you not like Chinese? Or is it the floats? You don't have to have any if you don't want to." I'm a little grumpy since he could have said something before. *It's not like he couldn't see what I was doing.*

"No, I like it all. I actually love root beer floats. Just haven't had anyone other than Apollo do something like this for me unless I ordered it from the kitchens." He has a funny look on his face that I can't quite decipher. Maybe something like embarrassment since he told me that or gratitude for the food. Deciding it's a mix of the two, I shrug it off like it's not a big deal, not wanting to embarrass him further, and continue filling my plate.

"Eat up before I get to it all. I can eat my weight in Chinese food." A wonton escapes as I'm putting it on my plate, and Marcus catches it before it hits the floor. Instead of putting it on my plate, he takes a bite, earning a scowl from me. With a laugh, he holds it up to my lips— I hesitate for a second, and he goes to withdraw— but I quickly open my mouth and take it from his fingers, nipping him a little in the process.

He inhales sharply, and I mumble an apology, turning my head away in embarrassment. He takes another off the baking sheet and nudges me to get my attention before he bites off it as well, bringing the other half up again for me to take. This time there's heat in his eyes, and I'm more careful, slipping my tongue out to lick the bit of left behind cream cheese off his finger. I blush at my actions, and I'm confused as well. I shouldn't like Marcus, but I kind of do. *This place is messing with my head.* He adjusts in his seat and sits back to start filling his own plate. With our plates full, we eat our food in companionable silence as we watch the antics on the screen.

"You like this movie?" He seems surprised when I nod my

head. We're almost finished with the movie and down to the bottoms of our floats when I hear a shout and a thump. I turn wide eyes to Marcus who goes to get up to investigate but stops when we hear Rex yelling at Braeden.

"Fuck, man! I didn't do it on purpose. Lark was between us when I fell asleep." I can't hold back the giggles this time, and Marcus stares at me again.

"What? It's funny. I got out of bed, and they slumped in toward each other. I was wondering when they were going to notice they were cuddling." Marcus shakes his head with a smile at my enjoyment of fucking with Rex.

"That's terrible, but funny too. I like when you laugh. We need to get you out of here so you have a reason to again." *Maybe Marcus really isn't all bad.* My thoughts are diverted as Braeden comes in, in a hurry, with Rex right behind him.

"Lark, damn it, wake me up next time! I thought something happened to you, and the human octopus was wrapped around me like Linus with his blanket." I bust up laughing again with Marcus joining in while both the guys glare at me. Finally getting ahold of myself, I apologize for laughing and scaring Braeden. As a peace offering, I offer to heat up some food for him, and I'm instantly forgiven at the mention of food he doesn't have to prepare himself.

We all settle in with food to watch the rest of the movie, enjoying the downtime that we have. Apollo and Brent find us that way as Emmett trails in still looking half asleep, crease lines on his cheek from the pillow and his wedge of badboy hair firmly in mussed territory— it's ridiculous how attractive he still is, even rumpled.

Apollo fiddles with his phone before setting it on the counter and nodding to Marcus. He's been doing it randomly and I'm thinking that's how he's letting us speak freely on occasion. My thoughts are confirmed when he starts talking.

"How are you feeling, Lark?" Apollo seems to be wary of

me, and I don't blame him. I should pop him in the nuts again, but I don't really see that he had an opportunity to do anything differently. *Hey, I can be rational.* Being trapped here is like being in an alternate reality, and I can't wait to get out.

"I'm fine." I don't say more than that, flicking my eyes towards Rex and Braeden. I don't want a scene, and neither of them is slow-witted, so they instantly pick up on it. Rex, of course, opens his big mouth.

"What really happened, Apollo? She's been abused enough, we need out now. I don't care about finishing the job." Rex has his fists clenched next to Braeden who looks thunderous. Marcus answers for him while Apollo stands there stone-faced.

"Restraints, flogging, figging, and fucking." Braeden's eyes get big, and Rex just looks confused. Marcus elaborates, "She got peeled ginger stuck in her ass, while she got paddled, and then Apollo had to fuck her in the ass too. All in front of his father and his cronies. It was the minimum that could pass as punishment and keep the others' hands off of her." Braeden glares at Apollo and comes to envelope me in his arms. I snuggle in, trying to decide what to say to take the worry from my friend.

"It wasn't as bad as it could have been. I'm embarrassed, and my ass is still sore, but I'm fine. I also agree with Rex, we need to get out of here before things escalate. Robert is seriously looking more and more deranged, and I don't even know the dude." I shudder a little when I remember him watching his son fuck me. Rex is pissed along with Emmett while Marcus looks sympathetic, and Apollo is still frozen.

With a sigh, I pull out of Braeden's arms and move over to Apollo. I pat his arm and quietly say it wasn't his fault. He glances down at me with those eyes, begging for forgiveness. "Really, Apollo, it wasn't your fault. Now, who's hungry? Because I'm not heating more food up after this." That seems to break the ice, and they all chime in with various yes answers, so I heat up everything that's left in the containers. After everyone is settled and eating, I sink down next to Braeden with Apollo on my other side. He seems shy or maybe humbled that I'm that close, but again, there really wasn't anything he could have done. I'd rather be alive and with these guys than dead or given to some other perverts that only want to cause pain for their own pleasure.

16

BLUE FUNKS AND BLOODY AUNTS

The days pass slowly— yet too quickly at the same time. There's still no word from the FBI go-between, making Apollo, Rex, and Emmett more worried as time goes on. As for me, I'm mostly in my own little bubble often staring off into space or napping. I hear Braeden whispering to the guys and Brent about it, but I refuse to have the doctor check me out. There's not anything he can do for it as I highly doubt they care about mental health or PTSD in here.

I'm lying on the couch with an upset stomach and barely react when Apollo comes in frantically, telling us about the national news station that picked up on my and Braeden's kidnapping. As of now, Rex and Emmett are the only suspects since there were cameras from other storefronts around the coffee shop showing the men going into the alley before Braeden and I followed a few minutes later. The investigators have concluded that we never came back out in that direction, and there wasn't any surveillance at the other end to see if there were others involved. A needle left at the scene with traces of a fast-acting sedative and my blood type was found, confirming I had most likely been incapacitated. He continues to go over the details of the news report while I stare despondently at the still image on the tv screen.

"Lark. Lark!" I startle out of my stupor to see what Braeden is yelling at me about. "Little bird, *what* is going on with you?"

I try to form a cohesive answer, but the words stick in my throat like glue. I settle on shrugging my shoulders, much to his displeasure. My abdomen is cramping and I'm sincerely hoping I'm not going to be sick.

"Brent, can you not help here?" Braeden directs his anger at the doctor.

"What would you like me to do? I can't force her to tell me what's going on, and I can't treat something I don't know the cause of." I idly note that the good doctor seems exasperated with us both.

I ignore the rest of the sniping between those two and the more serious conversation going on with the other four. Another cramp in my back alerts me to the issue that explains my stomachache; I'm going to have one of my infrequent periods. I'm not sure what to do about it, if there are even any supplies to be had. I get to my feet to make my way out of the room, heading for the bathroom. Wiping after I use the toilet, a light pink tinge is on the paper. I pull a few paper towels off the roll by the sink to fold them into my underwear for a makeshift pad.

After searching the cupboard in the hall, my shoulders slump in defeat— the shelves are bare of feminine products. Unless, of course, I want a douche. *Let's clean it out but not worry about periods. Assholes.*

Marcus steps up behind me as I close the cupboard door.

"Looking for something, Four?" Of course he's back to numbering me.

That's it, I can't take it anymore.

"My fucking name is *Lark,* you sadistic piece of shit!" Rapid footsteps come into the little hall at my shout— I now have a crowd to witness my meltdown. "Get away from me. All of you." Turning my back on the dumbfounded men, I stalk into the bedroom, slamming the door behind me. I throw myself on the bed, giving into my tears. The helplessness that over- whelms me follows me into troubled slumber.

Braeden

"I DON'T UNDERSTAND. She was fine. Well, as fine as she could be, considering the situation. She won't talk to me, and the more I try, the more upset she gets." Pinching the bridge of my nose, I wrack my brain for what could have set her off while the others stare at each other like lost idiots.

"This isn't my fault. I've already told you, multiple times, that I can't magically pull a solution out of my ass." *He certainly could if I shoved my foot up it.* Getting the gist of my thoughts from the expression running across my face, Brent shuts up and walks away.

Rex, ever helpful, states the obvious. "She's in there crying— again. Either she's crying, or she's yelling at us to leave her alone. That is, when she's not staring off into space, blocking everyone else out."

Sighing in disappointment, I go back to the living room area to give Lark her space.

Later that evening, when she still hasn't come out of the bedroom, my patience runs out. I have to piss, and I'm sure the others do as well. I open the door to find her a sleeping lump in the enormous bed. Not wanting to wake her, I go ahead and quietly use the bathroom, throwing the paper towel in the trash after I wash my hands. I happen to glance down and find blood-soaked wads of paper in it and nearly panic before comprehension dawns on me. I quietly go back out and through the bedroom to the hall, closing the door gently so as not to disturb her.

~

Emmett

"I'LL GO GET her some things. Do you know what she prefers?" Apollo's question is directed at Braeden.

I can't believe they hadn't bothered to have basic necessities on hand. It's no wonder she's so pissed. I voice my thoughts to the men gathered around the living room.

"You think being without supplies might be something like being stuck on the pot without toilet paper?" At least they have the grace to look ashamed.

"She shouldn't even be having a period. I mean, yes, there can be breakthrough bleeding, but it's not common after the first year. I was under the impression that Lark had been using the depo injection for a long time. If she'd cooperated and answered my questions, I could have let Marcus know to expect it. I need more medical history than she's willing to give me." The good doctor just doesn't know when to shut the fuck up.

Braeden proves that immediately, replying, "Are you really trying to blame her for having a period? Or for not divulging every little thing about herself?" Braeden's a big guy, and he's headed straight for Brent. If I'm annoyed with the doctor, he's probably livid.

Rex tries to grab his arm and gets pushed away. Marcus, shorter than them both, but no less built than Braeden, gets between them holding his hands up.

"I'll go. I'll get some of everything I can find. Can you three behave if I take Apollo with me? He needs to be seen regularly to avoid anyone coming here."

We all nod in the affirmative, retaking our seats around the room. They aren't gone long and come in with Marcus toting a large bag of feminine products and different pain relievers as well as a heating pad. Almost immediately, Braeden gets up and starts gathering things in his arms. He's able to pick out what she's likely to want even though I'm positive they have separate bathrooms in their home. I wonder if Lark knows how much of a stalker her best friend is. She probably wouldn't care, but still. I interrupt when he goes to leave the room.

"I'll take it." Expressions around the room vary from disbelief to annoyance. I explain my reasoning, "I'm the only one here that hasn't hurt her or badgered her incessantly about her issues. One of you goes in there, and she's going to blow up again."

Braeden reluctantly agrees, relenting, while Rex lets me know he's annoyed because he thinks it should be him before me. I'm going to have to explain again to my friend and partner about the breaking up thing. Apparently, he's extremely dense in this regard— or in denial.

TAKING THE ITEMS FROM BRAEDEN, I make my way to the bedroom, passing Marcus who's storing the leftover choices in the hall closet. I find Lark still curled up under the blankets and settle onto the foot of the bed on the corner opposite her. Watching her sleep, I memorize her familiar features. It hurts to know I helped drag her into this mess. It's unfair for her *and* Braeden.

Not long after I sit down, she begins to stir. Cracking her pretty brown eyes open, she flinches in surprise. "What are you doing? Stop staring at me. I swear you're such a sketchy asshole."

"Well, hello to you too, hellcat." I smirk at her narrowed eyes. *Oh, she doesn't like that nickname.* I remind myself to use it often. We excel at shooting barbs at each other.

"Which one sent you in here? You know you're the sacrifice, right?" She sits up, pulling herself backward to watch me better.

"I was a volunteer. I even edged your sidekick out. Here." Reaching down to the floor, I pick up the boxes and heating pad, placing them on the bed. "Think you're probably needing one or two of these."

She turns beet red, and I'm thinking it's more in anger than embarrassment. Yep, definitely anger.

"Did the manly men all get together to handle my problem?"

Well, the woman is spot on there.

"Oh, just hush and go to the bathroom."

She blinks at me in shock at the motherly type of command but gets up, grabbing the boxes anyway. It only takes a moment for her to recover and flounce indignantly off to the connecting room. I have to stifle a chuckle at her attitude since I don't want my balls smacked like I heard about Apollo getting. At least she's in better spirits when she returns. Sort of.

"Why you? And why do you always have to stare at me?"

I'm amazed she's noticed. I've always gotten the impression she mostly ignores me. "I like you, but I can never say anything that doesn't annoy you. And I figured I'm the least likely to take your insults personally. You always snipe at me. I'm used to it."

She doesn't react the way I expect her to.

"Well, thanks. I appreciate it. And I'm sorry if you think I'm always rude to you."

From the crestfallen expression on her face, I can tell she means it, and I feel like an ass pointing it out. Maybe I *should* have let Braeden handle it.

"Truce?" Sticking out my hand, I wait until she slips her smaller one into it before yanking her onto the bed with me.

She makes a chirping noise I can't help but laugh at. In a well-executed move I'm assuming Rex taught her, she flips over, straddling me. It's no wonder she's managed to hold her own in the physical altercations.

"Laugh at me again, and I'll tickle you so bad you'll pee your pants," she threatens.

Of course I can't help it and laugh at her again, earning little poking fingers digging into my ribs. I really am ticklish and try to squirm away by rolling. That works for all of two seconds until she manages to get one of my feet pulled back and an arm around my throat. I'm immobilized by the scrappy woman, and there's not a damn thing I can do about it without her choking me out. I'm crying 'uncle' with her knee drilling into my back when the bedroom door swings open.

Five sets of curious and worried eyes greet me, witnessing my downfall to the female on my back.

"Nightingale, is there a reason you're trying to kill him?" Apollo looks like he can't decide if he should be amused or come save me. *Wait, when did he start using a pet name?* Jealousy rears up in me, urging me to stake my claim on my wildcat.

"I think she should keep him there for a bit. She's been wanting to kick his ass since he called her bird butt." *Huh, I'd forgotten about that.* I throw a glare at Braeden. He's not helping me here.

Lark lets out a giggle at his comment. "Alright, all of you out."

Brent leaves right off, with the others slower to follow his retreat.

"Got something you wanna say to me, hellcat?" I yelp at her sharp little teeth sinking into the back of my neck. A chuckle outside the door lets me know at least one of the others stayed to eavesdrop. "What the hell was that for?"

"To remind you I bite. No more weird staring. And don't pretend you didn't like it. Pervert."

She's not wrong, I definitely didn't mind it. She climbs off me to yank the door open to a sheepish Rex and an unapologetic Braeden. Now, *that* rivalry is legendary. Not that Lark has ever believed her housemate carries a torch for her. Or noticed that I do as well.

17

GOING STIR CRAZY

Lark

The tussle and talk with Emmett, along with a tampon doing its job, relieve a great deal of my stress. I'm by no means great— or even fine. Any bit of reprieve is welcome, though. I'm also examining many of our past interactions in a different light. Unsure of how I feel about it all, I shelve it under 'things to deal with after getting out of crazy town'.

The guys are all gathered in the living room, minus the two currently getting the stink eye, arguing.

Marcus is protesting something Brent said that I hadn't heard.

"It's not safe. We can't protect everyone out there." I try to figure out what Marcus needs to protect us from.

"Everyone needs the exercise. And to get out of this tiny ass apartment. We're all going stir crazy and tripping over each other. I'm going whether anyone else does or not."

I deduce he's wanting to take us to a gym of some sort, and I agree with him. Even though the wrestling with Emmett has my brand burning, I'm itching to stretch my muscles, and a treadmill would be awesome.

"We're going. I'll try not to punch anyone. We can go at whatever time there's the least amount of people."

Narrowing his eyes at me, Marcus says, "That's half the problem. If someone gets handsy, neither you nor those three can do a thing about it. Brent and I can if it's a guard. Anyone else, and Apollo has to handle it. Even then he might not be able to intervene unless it's blatantly warranted. That's the other half of the problem. There are people at all hours, and they're not the best society has to offer. I'd know, I've been on the receiving end."

A frown marring his countenance, Apollo tries to come to a compromise. "We'll need to plan carefully and have an exit strategy, but I think we can make it work. I want you all to understand there are scenarios we can't anticipate. The responsibility for your choice is on you, I won't be held culpable for something outside of my control." A flick of his eyes toward me, and I know he's thinking of the brand and all that followed.

He's correct in assuming I still hold him responsible for that. A simple warning or any information at all regarding everything that's gone on would have gone a long way to avoid my ire.

THE FOLLOWING evening is our opportunity for escaping the boredom. Everyone that could cause large issues for us at the 'Facility'— as this place is known as— is at a party. Apollo filled us in some, and now we know that we're in the subterranean levels of an exclusive spa. He wouldn't tell us the name or the location, though I'm sure Rex and Emmett know, and I don't fuss about it. I want out of these rooms too badly to care. He did tell us it's a high-end place and even the upper-level guards will be gone, posing as security— leaving only the ones that he can order about if needed. A plan begins to unfold in my head. I keep my mouth shut until I can devise exactly how I want it to go.

Apollo goes over the rules one more time.

"No talking unless you need assistance. Only master," my nose wrinkles in displeasure, "or sir if you need to address Marcus or myself. If anyone touches you, come stand behind me. And *do not* hit *anyone*."

Nods from all of us spur Marcus to unlock the door and lead the way while Apollo takes the rear. I want to make an inappropriate joke about it, but I want to go on our excursion more.

We file our way silently down the hall, only the shushing of our footsteps accompanies us. We pass several closed doors and go around corners before we reach the gym. It's eerily silent even though I'm sure there is no way all those rooms aren't occupied. It's goes a long way toward showing how complete the soundproofing in this place is. Which should work to my advantage.

Entering a state-of-the art gym, I head directly for the treadmill, setting it to a near sprint. We're all dressed in t-shirts and shorts that we can easily move in. I'd already done my stretching while Apollo was going over his list of do's and don'ts. I roll my eyes at Rex and Braeden taking up the ones on either side of me. There aren't enough for all of us, and Apollo takes the last, leaving the other three to the ellipticals.

Sweating through my shirt a half mile in, my short breaths show the toll the inactivity has taken on my body. I push through to a full mile and walk on shaky legs to the rowing machine. I'll be damned if I don't at least finish a basic routine. The guys seem to fare better or at least hide it better, except for Apollo and Marcus. I'm sure they get regular workouts as I don't know where they go when they're not in the apartment with us.

By the time we're done, I'm soaked through and feel like my bones are the consistency of gelatin. *This is ridiculous.* Not to mention the irritating ass burn. The guys rarely remark on theirs, and as long as it's not infected— which Marcus checks for daily— I'm not going to complain. The water cooler stationed by the door is glugging away every time I refill the paper cup I'm using from the stack next to it.

"That's a five-gallon jug; if you keep trying to drink it all, you're going to get ill."

I flip my middle finger behind me in the direction the good doctor's voice comes from.

"Well, that's not very ladylike," he drawls.

Snorting mid swallow, I inhale a good amount of the water in my cup. The sputtering and choking I have going on brings my never far away crowd of men. *I need to get a girlfriend or two. There has to be a rule about the amount of attention allowed for male to female ratios.* I'm positive I've exceeded my fair share. Eyes and nose running and red-faced from embarrassment and coughing up a lung, I glare at Brent.

Voice croaky, I address him. "Take your ladylike expectations and shove them up your ass. Or maybe you'd be happier having one of them do it." Barb delivered, I stomp to the door marked as a bathroom.

It's worse than I'd imagined. My splotchy face, soaked hair, and shirt aren't at all attractive. Should deter anyone we might run into. Thoroughly done with the excursion, I go back out into the equipment-filled area to wait by the door. The guys take the hint I'm giving by ignoring them, and I'm grateful no one tries to talk to me.

Equipment shut off and put away, Marcus once again leads us out in the same formation we'd come here in. One turn around a corner away from our hallway, a keening filters down to us. I try to pick up the pace and get a restraining hand on my arm from Braeden. Apollo moves up the line around us all to go investigate.

In any other scenario, I'd think the noise isn't unusual; except here, the soundproofed rooms should have been blocking it. We follow Apollo albeit more slowly.

I wish I could say I'm shocked by what we come upon.

"Let her go." There's a burly man fucking a woman in the ass from behind. He looks up to snarl at the interruption but blanches when he sees Apollo, releasing the hand he has closed over the crying woman's mouth. Upon closer inspection, she's much younger than I'd originally thought, and I'm horrified and disgusted to witness it. She has a swollen face and eyes like she's been struck and blood on her thighs and bottom.

The guard tries to play it off like it's not a big deal. "She mouthed off. You know how they can get." And here it's probably not, unless you don't have permission to touch the merchandise. I'm going with he didn't obtain said permission in the first place based on the harsh lines that have taken over Apollo's aquiline features.

"Whose is she? I'll be escorting her back to her handler, put your dick away." I've seen him stern and blank faced; this is something else altogether. The hair raises on my arms, my body poised against the wrath emanating off him. I am very glad his anger isn't directed at me or my companions. Even Marcus appears wary in my peripheral vision.

The man's cock is hanging flaccid outside the placket of his pants. He slips it in, mess and all, before zipping up. Then the prick wipes his hand on the girl's back while she remains slumped over a utility sink. Apollo's isn't the only fist clenching in fury. The man cringes back, but it's too late. Apollo darts a hand out, gripping the man by his throat and tossing him out of the janitorial closet. He doesn't look back, just picks himself up off the floor to disappear down the hall.

I chance stepping forward, intent on helping the girl. Apollo zeroes in on my movements and seems to register that I'm not a foe as he focus' on my face. I edge around him, reaching for the bruised girl even as she shies away.

"Hey, hon. Come on, let me see where all you're hurt." The girl lifts a stark gaze in my direction, but she doesn't appear to be all there. She's been terribly traumatized, much like I would be right now had I not had the fortune of falling into the safer option. I don't want to force her to let me examine her with the guys. Although, Brent *would* be the better option if I was sure she would allow him near her. Stepping further into the small area, I motion Apollo out. "Could one of you please get something to cover her with? I think we should take her back to the rooms and check her out there. Anyone could come up on us here."

That shakes Apollo out of whatever state he's in, prompting him to send Marcus to get something to cover her with. Pulling the door shut, I flick the switch on the wall for a dim bulb to pop on, bathing everything in a yellowish light. Thankfully, the sink has hot and cold water, and with a few paper towels I wash the shivering girl up. She's starting to become more coherent and helps turn to allow me to reach other areas. I leave the spots between her legs alone except for in the most superficial manner. A shower would be best instead of scrubbing with rough paper. I try to make small talk to alleviate the tension.

"I'm Lark. What's your name?

The girl replies in a near whisper that is only audible because I'm so close. "Emily."

"Emily, how old are you? Do you know how long you've been here?"

"I just turned eighteen and graduated high school. I was at a graduation party the night I was taken. I think that was about two weeks ago." Emily's voice strengthens as she speaks.

My heart breaks for her being so young and innocent only to be caught like an animal. If there is ever a reason to not blow the guys' cover, *this* is a great one. I can't let this continue if I can help stop it.

A soft tap on the door sounds before it opens enough for a hand to slide a terry-cloth robe in. I take it, draping it around the girl and helping her get her arms in it. She moves stiffly, sore, I'm sure, from her ordeal.

When she's sufficiently covered, I open the door to lead her out, and she starts to panic at the sight of the group of males waiting for us. She must have not noticed them when we found her, and I reassure her the best I can.

"It's okay. They're friends of mine, they won't hurt you." She looks at me like I'm nuts. Not that I can blame her. I just hope my words are true in Apollo and Marcus' case as I don't know what all their duties entail.

I coax her out and down the hall, leaving Apollo to lead the way and the other guys to follow. I take her straight to the bathroom, closing the door on Apollo and Brent's surprised faces when they try to follow us in.

Apollo tries to protest through the barrier. "It's not safe, and Brent needs to look her over."

I know he could force the issue as there still isn't a lock on the door, but the fact that he doesn't, tells me more about what kind of person he is.

"If you think I can't handle one beaten female after you've seen what I'm capable of, you're not as smart as I thought you are. And Brent can check her after she's clean. Get her some painkillers, too, please." As I speak, I'm turning the water on in the shower. I see a small smile on the girl's face at my dressing down to the males outside. At least her spirit isn't completely broken after her mistreatment.

I help her get cleaned up, and most of her injuries seem to be superficial. She hisses at the showerhead when I direct it at her private parts, but they have to get clean too. I explain that Brent is Apollo's personal doctor and he'll be careful with her. That I'll stay with her the entire time. When she divulges a piece of information that infuriates me, I stalk out to the bedroom.

"She was a *virgin*!" Apollo has the grace to look away in shame. I shouldn't be surprised that this happens— and yet I am. And disgusted it hasn't been stopped sooner. Abruptly, Apollo pales.

"She's the new one Robert was in negotiations over. Fuck, he's going to flip out. We have to get her out of here. *Now*!"

I try to protest that she needs to be seen to by Brent, but he just keeps repeating she has to go, now. I shut my mouth and help her as quickly as I can into some yoga pants and a tank— apologizing profusely for being unable to help her— I barely get her hair brushed out before Marcus and Apollo hustle her out and disappear.

18

A HARD TRUTH

I t's hours before they come back, and I'm the only one still awake waiting.

They don't have the girl. Not that I'd expected them to. With disappointment in my voice, I ask, "What happened to her?"

Apollo motions with a finger to his lips for silence, before reaching into his pocket for his phone. After he taps the screen a few times, he glances at Marcus. He defers to him a lot, I'm noticing, in social interactions.

"She'll be seeing a doctor and going into general rotation like the pets you saw at the party. I'm not going to sugarcoat it, Lark." Yelling at him must have struck a guilty nerve because I'm honestly shocked that he used my name. "That girl was supposed to replace you. Her buyer wanted you after he saw you with all of us. He owns a stud farm in Ecuador and has certain—tastes." He finally finishes after searching for a word.

I wait for him to go on, and instead, Apollo picks up for him. *Guess it's too distasteful for even Marcus to talk about.*

"If he couldn't have you, he wanted a virgin to train himself. I didn't ask why, but I'm sure we can all speculate. When I refused to let you out of training for him to purchase, Robert appeased him with the girl." My hand slips up to cover my mouth in horror even as my eyes prick with tears. I hadn't known that poor girl was taking my place. "Now Robert is moving up the exhibition date yet again. Before the buyer leaves the country."

I stiffen legs that want to give out in weakness and terror. The urge to vomit is so bad I have to force down the saliva pooling in my mouth.

I'm being sold.

In a whisper, I ask the only thing that matters. "How long?"

Marcus, head down, mumbles, "Not long enough. Four days."

I shore up my ragged emotions, nodding. "I won't go. That's all there is to it."

Apollo's head jerks up. "Don't say that. Don't breathe a fucking word of that. You'll do whatever he says."

"The hell I will! Watch me." Arms crossed, I refuse to give in.

"He'll make you choose." I don't understand Apollo's meaning. "I had a brother once. He'll make you choose."

Marcus tries to stop him. "Apollo, no. We can't have you off the rails right now. Please. Master, for their sake."

My curiosity is piqued even with the dire conversation. I'd wondered if that was the relationship, but never heard Marcus address Apollo in such a manner.

Apollo holds up a hand to stop Marcus. "I'll be fine. Nightingale, here, has my full support. I won't jeopardize her safety." Turning his attention my way, he explains, "My mother wasn't technically a slave, but her father *did* sell her out, so she might as well have been. She was his trophy. Had all the etiquette classes, designer clothes, the works. He would trot her out to every social function. My father wasn't particularly loving, but he was civil... until my brother was born. He'd knocked up one of his pets. Made Mother take him in, pretend he was hers. She went into seclusion with the excuse of a difficult pregnancy, and no one was the wiser. She hadn't asked questions about where, or how, he earned his money, until my brother was six or seven. It was when Robert found out he had another child on the way. Another boy. Robert only allowed 'accidental' pregnancies to be kept if the child was male to continue his legacy. Later, I found out dear old dad had started shooting blanks more often than not. Thankfully, that meant my mother never had the misfortune of getting pregnant by him again. I suspect she'd have faced the same decree of an abortion, were it a girl. The pet had a stillborn toward the end of her pregnancy. Now, after being in seclusion, Mother now had to be in mourning for a child that wasn't hers.

She decided to take a spa week as that was acceptable society-wise. Except she hadn't told Robert, and it was one of his exhibition auctions. One of the members let it slip where she could overhear, and she went investigating. She knew he wasn't on the up and up but hadn't imagined what was really going on. She was horrified to find out and that he was grooming me to join in. I was fifteen by then and there to shadow him. He caught her trying to take my brother and I to leave him, and she refused to give in. He gave her a choice. She could continue to be a proper wife and keep her children, or she could leave. Without us. I think we all knew he'd never let her leave alive since he was a sadistic bastard even then. She attacked him with a knife she'd gotten from the kitchens, but she didn't get far before a guard stopped her. You've met him, Robert's assistant. My brother tried to help her, and it enraged Robert even more. Once more, he told her she had to choose. This time between her or my brother's life.

At that, I found my courage and protested. Robert cracked, spewing about breeding with common whores and ungrateful children. Mother refused to choose, and I don't blame her for what happened that night. Robert is insane. He took her stolen knife and slashed my brother's throat. Had me held by guards even as the one holding her back let go at a signal from him. He told her again to choose, and his assistant held a gun to my head just like he did Braeden's. My mother was on her knees, sobbing over my brother who had bled out in front of her, when she told me she loved me and used the knife on herself. I lost the two most important people to me that night and had to go on like nothing happened. An hour later, Marcus was escorted to my rooms as my 'present'. He was sixteen and captured from overseas. I was told to choose a symbol for my mark, and I did— he got a brand— while I got a tattoo."

Apollo looks at me with hollow eyes. "Now you know how monstrous we both are. Don't make the same mistake my mother and I made."

I don't have any words of comfort for him, but Marcus pulls him in, mumbling in a language I can't understand.

I make a decision; I'll get through Robert's debauched parade, and that's it. As soon as the guys are safe, either someone from the FBI or elsewhere intervenes, or I'll take care of it before I leave the States. It'll be me or my new owner— one of us won't make it past the border. I won't end up like the poor girl we found in the closet.

19

PRACTICE MAKES PERFECT

Lark

Apollo goes over the extensive list of requirements and works out a game plan. The first portion of the training list is up— double and triple penetration.

I make my way into the training room, the last to arrive. My skin is still sore from the full body waxing I received yesterday. *At least I won't have to worry about shaving for a while.* Everyone is here, even Brent. Marcus will be directing as usual. I'm nervous as I requested to forgo the drugs that make it easier to handle.

"You will all double up, but not complete that way. You can finish each other or yourselves off after your turn. There are two days left until the exhibition to run the gauntlet on that list. We can't take the chance of accidental injury beforehand."

Following his instructions, we all strip down. Since I've already tied my hair up, I get in the chair while Marcus takes the guys to line up on the wall next to me. Poles extend from the walls like checkmarks in between the rails I noticed the first time I was in here. "You four will stretch yourselves twice daily regardless of other activities. This will keep those areas limber."

Marcus has each guy straddle the poles facing the wall and then adjusts the pole's height. He brings a box and begins affixing black rubber dildos— all the same large size. "These will be standard, I'll show you where they're kept later. I'm sure you can all handle your own lubrication now. I'll leave three tubes and a bottle on each tray. Just ask if you need more. After each of you reaches full penetration, I'll start the counter. You'll start with fifty strokes. I modified some step counters with a sensor that your ass has to pass over to trigger. The counts will be on the screen right here so you can watch for being done. These are all eleven inches in length and eight inches in circumference. Get them in at your own pace and join us for Four's training when you are finished. Oh, and full removal will be necessary to complete the stroke, there's a sensor at the top too." That brings a groan from them all. With that, the guys are left to lube up and get started.

Marcus and Apollo are both going to be working with me. They're starting out with three tubes of lube in each hole and progressive stretching of width and depth. I'm sitting partially reclined with my legs open and knees bent high, getting the best exposure and angle. As the lube is applied, I watch the guys. Braeden and Emmett get their tubes popped in and out quickly and line up almost simultaneously on their dildos. Spreading their asses on the wet silicone, they get just the tip pressing on their holes before sinking down onto them. With slow presses forward and back, they're soon seated fully on them. I look over, and Brent and Rex are both about halfway— panting. I almost laugh at their expressions. They both kinda deserve it— Brent after that lovely first meeting, among other things— and Rex for the night we were kidnapped.

The finger-like trainers Marcus and Apollo are using are long. They're sliding them in one at a time as far as I can take them, then holding them pressed in with the opposite hand. They're marked for Braeden's length and counted out for Marcus' width. Marcus is working on my rear while Apollo takes my front. I had asked why not stretch them separately, but with one of the tasks on the checklist being taking Marcus and Braeden at the same time, Marcus said this will be most like that. By the third in each hole, my attention is mostly pulled away from the guys.

I hear Rex muttering that taking Braeden the first day hadn't been as bad as this, with Braeden retorting that he told him he took it easy on his ass. I think Rex finally believes him, and he must push down too hard because I hear him yelp again. This time I can't hold back the chuckle until Marcus matches Apollo for the fourth and starts working it in my now-filled anus. Marcus tells me once they get several in, they can place them in the center of the others so the edges of my openings aren't hurt by being pried at, just all the other sticks expanding outward. The fifth comes, and I'm afraid to move. I feel stuffed and still have three to go in each place.

They pause as a beep sounds with another following a few seconds later.

Apollo turns his attention to the guys. "Did you two have a race?" He sounds amused, and I'm not surprised to see that it's Braeden and Emmett.

I look fondly at Emmett now— after the last week we've grown close— and at least today, they'll be the first up. I groan as they resume with six. By the time they reach eight I almost sound like Rex did a few minutes ago, who's also finished now, and has come over to observe.

"Holy, shit." Is of course what comes out of his mouth when he sees me so full. *Dick.*

Eight makes it in my pussy, but my ass is rebelling and I'm panting at the pain. Marcus frowns at me.

"Four, are you sure you don't want the drug? It'll help take the edge off."

I shake my head. "No, I don't want it." I ignore him calling me Four again. He's explained, that even with Apollo using the hammer, they need to try to stay in character as much as possible to avoid slip-ups.

He sighs in defeat and turns to gets the tubes— slimmer than the rods he's using— filled with gel, and I eye them in trepidation. Pulling a rod out of each hole, I breathe a little easier. He picks up one tube, explaining when I balk, "It's only got lidocaine mixed in for numbing."

I nod and he applies it to the ring of muscle at the entrance before moving further in. Sighing with relief before he's even finished, I start to feel better. Two more of plain lube follow in my ass as well as three in my vagina. Finished, they both start twisting the rods and moving them back and forth, spreading the lubrication, and getting me worked up in the process.

The rod that was removed is replaced more easily, and slowly, my ass takes it. I get nine in my pussy without any pain — it's the last— even though Apollo has to work it in with effort. I see all the men have gathered and are staring at my crotch, palming their dicks.

Marcus goes for the center of the group in my backdoor but can't get it started. Braeden suggests pulling them all out half-way, together, spreading the ends so they're not grouped so tightly, and inserting it to the same depth, before then sliding them all in at once so it doesn't get hung up. They feel like one piece sliding out like that, and when the other rod sinks in, it spreads them out even more, making me gasp at the strain.

Before Marcus pushes them back in, Apollo gets a wand vibrator and starts rubbing it over my clit. Soon I'm getting into it, and Marcus starts pushing the rods in together. As he does, the vibrator on my clit kicks up a couple notches, and I moan while my pussy and ass spasm. My ass is spasming so much, and with the rods already being so far in and with pressure on them, they start sucking in on their own, making me arch and emit incoherent noises at the insane fullness and pinching pleasure I'm feeling.

Abruptly, much to everyone's surprise, I come hard. As I calm from my orgasm, I become aware of the desirous expressions around me. I'm slightly embarrassed, but then I remember I just watched them fuck themselves on dildos.

Marcus starts pulling out rods and throwing them in a basin to be washed later. As the last of them come out, I feel oddly empty and still slightly open. The guys are all staring— fixated— at the space between my legs. Marcus waves his hand forward, and that's all it takes. Rex drops to his knees and starts eating me out. Licking and sucking like his life depends on it I feel his tongue spear deep until he withdraws a minute later to carry me to the swing. With Marcus helping, I'm secure in minutes. It's disorienting to be in it. I can be in virtually any position while suspended with the height adjusted for whoever needs it. Braeden hangs back with Marcus. I know they'll be doing their thing together afterwards, and I get nervous goosebumps imagining it. Rex and Brent get in the two remaining swings, and Emmett and Apollo bring them closer on their tracks before Apollo tips me back into Rex's arms. He immediately starts to play with my tits, twisting and pulling at my nipples the way he knows I enjoy.

"Are you wet for me, baby?" he whispers in my ear. I nod my head yes, choosing— for now— to ignore our status as a non-couple. Emmett comes up to me with something held behind his back.

"I think she likes that, Rex, but she's going to like *this* even more." It's now become a competition as to who can get the best reaction from me. I feel something cold and slick probe my entrance. Trussed up in the straps of the swing like I am, absolutely everything is on display and easily accessed. It sinks in about an inch and is decently wide. At that point I feel another wet probe on my other entrance, and I tense some in nervousness.

"Relax, baby, you'll like it. I promise." Promises from Rex are honored until it suits him differently, I'm sure. He starts rolling my nipples instead of pulling on them and brings his head down to lightly bite the space between my neck and shoulder. He knows that's a hot spot for me, and I moan, distracted as he'd obviously intended.

While I'm busy trying to remember why I'm mad at Rex, the second object penetrates me. It's thinner than the one in front, but not by much. I feel stretched and very turned on. As both pieces move up into me, I feel little rubbery strings that are slightly stiff tickle across my clit. Once the toy is seated fully, the base of those strings is pressed under it where it's extra sensitive, and then they come up, surrounding it in a vee shape.

Emmett does something, resulting in a click, and my ass comes alive with vibrations. Another click, and what feel like small beads begin to spin inside me. The third click brings the strings around my clit to life. Emmett grinds it against me, rolling it in a tight circle. I'm moaning in pleasure in minutes, and right before I come again, he pulls it out.

Apollo slides Brent up to me in his harness, placing his dick in line with my pussy and using the movement of the swings to impale me on it. Apollo stays behind Brent and— reaching around— grabs my hips and pulls me on and off Brent rapidly, using him to fuck me. I feel Rex pressed up against my back as his hands settle on my tits again.

"Don't worry, baby, we all get to relax and go for a ride. Apollo and Emmett are going to handle everything." Rex and his 'baby' shit is pissing me off, regardless of my earlier intent to get along.

Apollo stills Brent before I can go off on Rex, and I notice fingers, gloved up, on my anus. Since everyone else's are busy, I'm assuming it's Emmett that slicks lubricant over it then in me before moving to Rex and guiding his dick to my empty hole. He'll be the second I actually take in the ass; from anal virgin to multiple partners in days.

"Emmett, be careful with her," Rex warns him. I feel a little more charitable toward him for at least caring about my comfort.

Getting behind us both, Emmett reaches up between Rex's legs to take control over his cock and keeps it steady as he pushes Rex into me. It's slow going, and it burns and hurts at first, but eventually we get there. Opening my eyes, I see Brent staring at me in an affectionate way, and it kinda wigs me out. *Guy is always so hot and cold, nice one minute and a jerk the next.*

Rex and Brent grunt almost simultaneously, and when I crane my head to look, I realize they're going to get fucked into me as they're buggered themselves. Emmett pulls Rex out before reseating him to the hilt— repeating this several times— before both he and Apollo begin moving Rex and Brent in careful tandem.

Rex and Brent are pushed in and pulled out of me while they're impaled on Emmett and Apollo. Marcus doesn't want anyone getting too excited and tearing someone up, but I'm about to come again if anyone so much as touches my clit. Marcus must have read my mind as he comes up, bringing his hand between me and Brent to pinch and pull at it. He begins rubbing in circular motions, and that's it. I'm clenching ass and pussy on the cocks in me, dragging moans from them both. Before they can come too, Marcus separates everyone—much to the displeasure of Rex and Brent who are vocal about blue balls.

"There's more training. Four is mostly done for now, but you four still have more to go. I'll have her assist me. Being horny will help you with it unless anyone wants the drug. I can give you just a little to take the edge off." Marcus waits for anyone to take him up on his offer, and no one does. "Emmett, I want you to take this one. You need more experience with receiving. I'll get you all set up with the equipment."

WHILE HE LEADS them all over to the stocks contraption, Braeden goes to the chair closest to it and reclines, adjusting the knees and footholds I'll use while straddling Marcus. I climb up on him, both of us naked, and try to ignore the erection brushing against me. I hover just over him and avoid making eye contact, instead watching the other guys. Braeden doesn't let it stay awkward for long though.

"So, pretty bird, ever think we'd be fuck buddies? I mean, how many times did Rex think we were doing it, anyway? We could have totally been shacking up and boinking like rabbits the whole time." I look at him and drop my forehead to his with a helpless giggle.

"I never even knew you could get it up for a girl, Brade. You never told me, so I never thought of you as other than my hot best friend." And I really didn't. Of course I knew he was attractive, I'd have to be dead not to know that, but he was so much more than a pretty face and a hot bod.

"I don't know about *any* girl, love bird," he almost whispers. I look at him sharply, realization dawning on me. The short-term boyfriends, all the cuddling, and Rex always having an issue with our physical closeness as well maybe should have been clues, but I'd been oblivious.

"Not here, Brade. When we're home, okay? And for the record, I don't mind my best friend throwing me a bone. In the ass or not." I wink at him before peeking around to see that the others are still occupied and give him a peck on the lips to lighten my words. We both fall silent and turn to watch Emmett.

The contraption must have had to be adjusted as Marcus is locking some part of it down and telling Emmett to try it now. He looks nervous, and I see why when he gets in it. His upper chest is on a padded bar, and his chin on a rest with his arms drawn behind him into the boards and locked back. His knees come up next to his hips with his ass fitting through a cutout, and his feet are locked into more boards on either side of it. He's through it far enough that his testicles are pushed up along with his penis towards his stomach, just his buttocks and scrotum showing through the circle. Marcus speaks again to everyone.

"As you all know, we're trying to knock out as many tasks in multiples as we can off that list to limit everyone's exposure to others. This will satisfy a bondage, a gag, a spanking, a DP, and a pegging. For the actual event, Four will be performing the pegging and whipping as she's the only female we have. I could ask another female, but I don't want that to be taken as anyone can be substituted or loaned out. Four, we'll practice later. For now, just get a feel for it."

Apollo is wielding what he explains is a riding crop, and Rex has a thick metal rod with a rounded top specifically made for penetration. Rex covers it in lubrication before applying more to Emmett's ass liberally. Brent is palming his dick, keeping it hard while Marcus fits a metal framed ring into Emmett's mouth after checking that it fits over Brent's dick and lining the back of Emmett's teeth with a thin rubbery membrane to protect them. The circle portion goes behind them holding his mouth wide while the sides, that resemble metal triangles come off it and curve around his cheeks like a head halter attached to a velcro strap that tightens it all down.

Locked in as he is with his chin on a rest and mouth forced wide, it will be Brent controlling the movement. I'm tingling all over down low, and my nipples have hardened, I almost wish I was in it instead. I've definitely gotten dirtier and more adventurous sexual leanings since I've been here. Braeden must be enjoying the anticipation as well, as I feel his dick pulse against me. Marcus checks everything over before nodding for them to begin.

Brent fits his dick in the ring and feeds it into Emmett's mouth, reaching the back of his throat and holding onto the frame as he pushes deeper, almost gagging Emmett, until a loud crack sounds that makes Emmett twitch and yelp. When Emmett's throat opens for the sound to come out, Brent is able to push in farther, sliding balls deep. The crack of leather on flesh continues as Apollo wields the crop on Emmett's pale cheeks, successively one after another. They begin hitting his scrotum and anus as well causing Emmett to moan and shake. I think he likes it. Brent is going all the way in and out in controlled thrusts, dragging strings of spit with each movement as Emmett can't swallow well around the gag. Apollo pauses and begins massaging his buttock, and Rex steps up with the rod. Apollo spreads Emmett wide, and Rex begins pushing in. The round tip quickly disappears as Rex works it in until he hits the base then backs out. Emmett is groaning, twitching, but he can't move. Nodding in approval, Marcus leaves them to it, coming over to me and Braeden.

"THREE, I want you in the rear. I don't think there will be a preference on the order of who is in what hole other than the biggest two. I don't want to damage her ass with my width. If it comes to it, we'll deal, but you're big enough to make me worry already." We both get up from the chair, Marcus taking Braeden's place and me climbing up on him. I'm still slightly uncomfortable being physical with him, but I try to ignore that. I'm also acutely aware Braeden can see everything behind me,

I fit my legs back into place and hover my crotch over his. He reaches between us, and slides his finger through my swollen wetness, seeming slightly surprised I'm so wet. He slides a finger in, pumping, then two, working me up further. He withdraws and lines up with my opening, pulling me down onto him. It's a stretch, but once he's gotten it started, I rock and wiggle until I'm fully seated. I open my eyes, not realizing I'd closed them, to find a look of intense lust staring back at me from Marcus' face. I blush, knowing he can tell from the little movements that I'm enjoying him in me.

I hear Braeden come behind, and he soon enters me with a slicked finger working in and out. It's more intense with the size of Marcus in me than it was with Brent. Out of all of them, he and Rex have the smallest dicks, but that doesn't mean they're objectively small at all. They're above average, but these others are just freaks of nature. *I got saddled with the big dick posse.* I giggle at the thought, and all I can do is shake my head when Marcus asks what's so funny. *I'm not sure either man would appreciate my humor.*

Braeden's added a finger and is stretching me with them. He adds more lube, a different one than before. It's clingy, almost like a slimy glue. Straight up, it looks like gobs of my fluids after I've come, but thicker. He presses me down tightly onto Marcus, who locks his arms around me like I'm going to try to escape.

"Relax as much as you can, it'll be easier to take if you don't fight it. Oh, and bear down some like you're trying to go to the bathroom. It will help open those muscles." Marcus almost seems concerned. I wonder if they're having a silent conversation over my head, but I'm too nervous to try to find out.

I watch Emmett taking the rod like a jack hammer now as

his back is being lashed with the crop and underneath to hit his cock and balls. Brent looks like he's concentrating on not blowing his load yet. I'm lost in the scene but quickly pull back to my own reality when I feel the head of Braeden's dick touch my asshole. As he leans forward, I push back and flex my sphincter, trying to get it to accept him. I start whining in my throat and tense against my best attempts not to.

"I can't," I yell into Marcus' chest, close to tears. It fucking hurts so bad. We have everyone's attention now. Marcus waves for them to continue and tells Braeden to get the wand vibrator for him. He has me sit up some and fits it between us against my clit, starting it on a low setting. My asshole still feels tender, but the vibrations are helping, and I'm beginning to relax. I feel yet more lube applied and try to stay relaxed, but it's difficult with the memory of that burning pain so fresh.

Braeden lines his head up again with my throbbing hole and pushes until I'm just slightly broken open. It's not particularly comfortable, but it doesn't burn either. Just holding pressure there, he must signal to Marcus because the pace of the vibration picks up. Immediately, my anus pulses and lets Braeden slide in a smidgen. With each pulse of my ass, he's let further in, but as soon as he's almost through the tight ring of muscle I begin to feel the full stretch and start tensing at the hideous pressure. The vibrations go up several levels, and I bear down harder, letting him in steadily.

I begin to make mewling noises, grasping at Marcus' shoulders. When Braeden stops, I breathe a sigh of relief, thinking he's done as he draws backward. No such luck. The vibrator goes on its highest setting as Braeden pumps back and forth just that little bit. I start to grind down, that feeling of arousal returning with a vengeance. I turn my head to Brade and see his face tighten into a grimace, that and the fact that I can see his hand around his dick while he's in me, alerts me to the fact that he didn't reach full depth. I reach back and grab his thigh, pulling him to me. He looks at me with a question in his eyes, and I nod. He moves back into his previous depth and keeps going. I feel like I'm going to break in two when he finally moans and reaches the end, balls tight up against me and Marcus both.

They both hold still until the vibrations get to me, and I attempt to move, but they both just hold me there, tight and stuffed, until I begin to come. I lightly moan into Marcus' chest as I spasm over them both, causing Braeden to spread my cheeks wide and grind against my asshole. I'm becoming too sensitive, and Marcus removes the wand and sets it aside. I'm nearly limp, and they both take advantage of that as they begin an alternating pace. One in, one out, and every third or fourth rotation they both push back in together.

I'm enjoying the overfull sensation and watching the show next to me. The rod has been discarded, and Apollo is nailing Emmett in the ass while Rex and Brent take turns putting their dicks down his throat. Pulling back and jacking off after pulling out of Emmett's throat, Brent blows first, spurting and aiming for the gagged mouth he's been plundering. Most of it ends up on his tongue, but some hits his cheeks and chin, and it's all dripping everywhere. Rex doesn't pause a beat, leaning down and licking Emmett's lips before standing and filling his mouth and throat again. Apollo has his eyes closed, pumping away, then suddenly pulling out and holding Emmett's ass open to slow down the contraction of his stretched ring. He strokes his length a few times and lets loose all over Emmett's open hole. While he's still ejaculating, he pops back in with a groan from Emmett and finishes off.

Up front, Rex pulls out of his mouth and pushes Brent to his knees before burying his cock in his mouth. Brent starts sucking for all his worth as he tries to take Rex's deep thrusts. Suddenly, Rex stills and backs up enough for Brent to suck him dry and swallow, licking him like a lollipop until he's clean.

Apollo has released Emmett, who's sporting an impressive hard on. Apollo leads Rex to the pommel bench and lubricates his backdoor. Emmett is so worked up he barely pauses after sliding the head of his dick past the opening before sliding in fully. He pushes in and pulls completely out three or four times, exposing Rex's pink tunnel each time before burying himself to the hilt, stilling with his orgasm and leaving the mess inside Rex. He pulls back, and Rex slowly gets to his feet. I can see the fluid starting to seep back out and down his thigh. That was short and intense, but I'm not surprised Emmett came so quickly after all he'd just been through.

I'm so turned on by what I saw that I'm ready to come again. Up until now I let the guys move. Experimentally, I swivel my hips in a slow circle and nearly see stars as the steel-like cocks in me hit every spot. I continue to do that until Marcus brings the wand back, and Braeden picks up his pace. Apollo comes up behind Braeden and kneels. I feel a tongue running all over my plugged holes and the space in between them. A finger comes up and probes at my pussy, then the tongue disappears along with the finger, I hear Braeden groan and hear sucking noises. I can imagine Apollo sucking on his balls and entering him with the finger I just felt. Another finger probes around, coating itself in the liquid dripping from me before sliding past me and leaving Marcus sharply moaning. Braeden's thrusting becomes erratic, and as he starts to come, the pulsing of his dick in my ass pushes me over the edge, and my own contractions drag Marcus swearing and groaning with us.

We finally settle after Apollo stops licking and withdraws, and Braeden very carefully disengages from me, then helps me lift up off Marcus. He doesn't even put me down, and I'm glad as I don't think I can walk right now, and carries me directly out and to the bathtub.

I have cum leaking from both holes onto his arm, but he

doesn't seem to care. He sits me down, keeping an arm around me as he adjusts the water, before swinging me back up into his arms. I feel cherished, and I hold on tight around his neck. When the water is partially full, he climbs in still holding me and lowers us both to the bottom.

20

A MAD PLAN

He begins washing me while still cradling me. Surprisingly, I'm not uncomfortable being with him like this. He's been my best friend since high school, and now I think we might end up being more. *If we ever get out of here.* Honestly, the thought of any of them at this point not getting out with me brings on a panic just to think about. Even the assholes I don't particularly like most of the time. I push off that line of thinking and gather my energy to move from his lap. I can wash myself even if it is nice that he's helping. I need to know that I am able to hold myself together and not rely on anyone if I have to. Braeden has a bit of a hurt expression on his face, but I smile at him gently and reach out to rub his shoulder. The hurt changes to confusion, but at least he's not upset. I don't want to explain it.

I dip my head in the water and quickly wash and condition my hair. At least I don't need to shave again, that would be awkward with company in the bath. Shaved stubble floating around in the tub water and getting stuck to bodies is not attractive or probably particularly sanitary. I go to get out as the others file in and start heading for either the tub or the shower. Braeden gets out and drains it, so it can be filled with clean water. I leave the bathroom to get dressed, deciding to come back for a hairbrush and deodorant later.

After everyone is clean and dressed, we lounge around the living room while Apollo and Marcus go for more 'take-out'. I swear the kitchen here must have one of those chain buffets in it like the Golden Corral or something. Settling on the couch with Emmett and Rex on either side, and Braeden on the floor in front of me, I relax as Brade rubs my feet and lower legs. I let out a soft moan when he hits a sensitive spot and open my eyes to Rex and Emmett staring.

"Really, guys? It felt good. I'm not having sex with either of you outside what I have to. Not to mention I'm not sure how you could even be interested right now. Even if my shit didn't feel like it was a tenderized steak, I still don't think I'd be in the mood. I'm pretty freaking worn out." I kind of feel bad after I see the effect my words have on them. "Well, crap. Sorry, guys, I'm a little strung out, I think."

Surprisingly, it's Emmett that reaches out to put his hand on my arm. "It's alright, Lark. We don't blame you, I think we're all a little strung out. Come on and snuggle in, we aren't about to jump your bones." With that, he tucks me in under his arm like he's been doing when he's being friendly, and I'm surprised to realize I'm quite comfortable. Rex also cuddles in by laying his head in my lap. I sigh and let myself enjoy it instead of kicking him.

"Emmett?" I'm nervous about bringing this up, so I don't even attempt to look at him, "I'm not going to break without you all holding me together. I don't want you to think it's your responsibility to take care of me or that you have to be affec-tionate just because we're being forced to have sex." I get quieter as he stiffens next to me, and I brave a glance up. Rex and Braeden are also doing impeccable impersonations of statues. I think they all know something I don't. Emmett takes a deep breath and then speaks.

"It's not that I don't or even didn't want to in the past, hell-cat. I just felt it would be over stepping boundaries. And frankly, it wouldn't matter if we weren't having sex, I'd still comfort you." I'm confused, but I don't push it.

That is until Brent opens his big fat mouth. I hadn't realized he was eavesdropping in the kitchen area.

"He's got the hots for you, smart one. I swear, you're seriously oblivious, or just in denial about the men around you. It's not appropriate to cop a feel, even innocently, from your buddy's girl." I'm gonna smack him. Maybe I'll chuck one of those giant dildos at him again. He's embarrassed Emmett, and that isn't very nice. Maybe I *am* in denial, but he could have been more tactful.

"Could you be any more of an ass? I swear you like being a prick. It's fine, Emmett. In the effort for full disclosure, I thought you were hot too. Doesn't mean I would have acted on it," I add when I get the stiffy effect going on around me again. "I'm not blind, you guys. Rex, I wouldn't have cheated on you or anything like that either. Now I'm not saying I wouldn't have gone for a threesome or two—" I trail off again at the shocked faces. "What?! You can't *really* be surprised by that. You *have* seen what he looks like, right?" I'm talking to Rex directly at the end since he's looking a little grumpy.

"I'm not mad. I'm just thinking that I should have asked a long time ago, and I'm kicking myself for not doing it." I laugh at that one. I can definitely see him being cranky about missing out.

"Alright, so now that that's out of the way I'm napping until the other two come back with food." I shut my awkward mouth and put my head on Emmett's chest, soon lulled to sleep by his steady, if a tad rapid, heartbeat.

I awake to low male voices again. *This is becoming a theme.*

Without opening my eyes to check, I'm pretty sure it's Apollo. I'm getting fairly familiar with their voices.

"The exhibition has been moved up. It's tomorrow night. I've left a message for my contact. I just hope he understands it when he receives it. I don't want to worry any of you, but if this goes south, you'll be sold tomorrow and separated and shipped out the following morning. I can't stall that. That's also *if* you aren't claimed by buyers tomorrow night afterwards. The only rule that has to be abided by is all acts must be complete before bidding begins. Even those with prior buyers have to wait for the first options to be given. There's always a chance that a buyer changes his or her mind, and then the merchandise goes up for auction." Fully coming awake, the panic sets in; shallow breaths and a rapid heart rate cue Emmett in that I heard the conversation. He takes up rubbing small soothing circles on my back in reassurance.

"Don't worry, hellcat," he whispers, "we'll make it out. We have trackers to implant for all of us tonight. In case we get separated we'll be able to find everyone. No matter what, stay safe and cooperate. We'll come for you." Worry sits heavily in his tone.

Tipping my head back to peek up at him, I find him gazing down at me with a furrow between his eyes. "No checking out on us, alright? You're a fighter, don't give up now." He speaks too quietly for the others to notice. This is only between us.

"I'll try," is all I can offer him. Making an effort to stay calm, I manage to drift back off. Relatively safe for now.

WHAT I THINK IS a short time later, I wake up. No windows really messes with gauging the time in here. I'm in bed between Emmett and Braeden, and the others are nowhere to be seen.

Remembering that the day is moved up, I nudge Emmett. I have an idea, and I'll need him for it.

He bolts up, startled. "Chill, everything's fine." He relaxes, flopping back onto the bed. "Sshhh, geez you're gonna wake Braeden up," I whisper.

"Too late, Braeden is already awake," the man in question interjects.

"Fine, whatever. I have an idea I think Emmett can help me with. Remember the whips?"

Braeden chuckles while Emmett answers, "How could we forget the whips?"

Rolling my eyes at them, I explain, "I want Emmett to be my cigarette girl. I'll train him as much as possible now, and that'll give us weapons and a reason to have them. It'll be a novelty that, hopefully, no one will question. It can be our last act." I'm optimistic that if things go sideways, I'll be able to defend myself.

Half-baked plan in place, we get up and dressed to go find the others.

Rex is asleep on the couch when we exit the bedroom, but the door to the training room is propped open. At least one of the others is in there. Upon entering the room, my steps freeze; Brent is hovering over Marcus' back which is covered in welts, rent flesh, and in several places, blood. My swift intake of air is enough to alert them that they'd been intruded on. Marcus tries to quickly move off the exam chair he's resting against, but the abrupt move causes him to grunt in pain and one of the plastic strips Brent was using to pop loose, letting the cut bead up and run over with bright red blood. Marcus tries to kick me out, probably not realizing I'm not his only company.

"Lark, out!" *What happened to Four?*

I snort. "Right, and since when have I listened to your grumpy ass? And what the hell happened to your back?" Before he can answer, I realize we're missing a person. "Where's Apollo?"

Silence ensues for a moment, and I think he's not going to answer. I can feel the heat of the guys from behind me, causing a small shiver to work its way across my skin. Whether it's from muscle memory of being in this room or the lower temp isn't clear. Probably a combination of both.

"He's in the shower back there." Marcus tips his head toward the nearly seamless door I'd wondered about before. *An extra bathroom would have been nice to know about.* "Washing the mess off, I'd imagine. As for my back— Apollo happened. Or rather, *Robert*. He forced Apollo's actions by questioning who was in control— me or him. You should be able to fill in the blanks from there." His matter-of-fact explanation reeks of suppressed anger and pain.

Brent stays silent while curses and jostling happen behind me; the guys are pissed. Braeden stalks toward the hidden bathroom, intent clear in his attitude.

"Braeden, no." I rush to get in front of him.

Apollo chooses that moment to come out, steam escaping from the door around him. Dressed in a pair of gray sweats and barefoot, he's rubbing a towel on his head when he notices his silent audience. A tightening in the corner of his mouth and a short nod are the only signs he gives that he knows what he did was wrong.

Braeden makes no move to follow him as he goes to go check on Marcus. It's a private moment I feel we're all intruding on when Apollo rests his forehead on top of Marcus' head.

To distract the others, I get us back on track to the purpose of our visit to the room. Going to the cupboard where I'd found the whips before, I reach in to select several. Freezing mid motion, I remember that Marcus was most likely up close and personal with one not too long ago. I shake off the hesitation since much worse than a beating can, and has, happened here.

I go over my thoughts again and catch the attention of the others. Even Rex has wandered in now, sleepy face still going on as he heads straight to Apollo and they take up a low conversation.

I do the best I can to instruct Emmett. By the time we're done, he can at least wield it. The last bit of time I use for target practice and a few runs of snapping straws from between his lips. It takes three tries before he didn't flinch backwards. I ignore Rex's muttered, "Damn, that's hot," but the others get on him for it. Apollo worries that it might be too attention garnering with Robert, but ultimately, he admits it's a smart way to defend myself.

With twelve hours until the party begins, Apollo and Marcus herd us all to bed and showers.

NEED A HAND?

(PREVIOUSLY DELETED SCENE)

Lark

"Why do we have to do this? And why me? Can't one of you take it up the ass instead? This fucking two holes thing and you always wanting to fill them is getting old." I'm plain pissed off. Yet again, my legs are up in the stirrups as I await the newest form of erotic torture. I almost feel sorry for Emmett who is staring back and forth from my bare center to his gloved hand and back again with trepidation clear on his face while Marcus pumps the ever-present gobs of lube over it, but he's not the one it's going to be stuffed into.

"Unless someone is volunteering, yours is the only vagina available. Besides, it's made to stretch out." I'm going to shank his ass the first chance I get.

I eye the others that are surreptitiously trying to watch without outright staring. There's no doubt they're interested, or at least their dicks are since they're all either bobbing in the wind or tucked up against their bellies. As I'm about to snap at them to find something else to do besides study me like a bug under a magnifying glass, Apollo rescues me.

"Marcus, I can take over here. Why don't you go get the others dressed?"

The man in question studies Apollo for a moment before nodding and turning to direct the rest of the guys to the other side of the room. He quietly says on his way past, "Don't make her a target when we're out there. Remember, they're always watching."

Apollo nods, grim faced, and flicks an apologetic glance my way before pulling up a stool and getting entirely too close to my crotch. The man seriously has a fascination with pussy. You'd think he didn't get to see enough of it in his line of work with the way he focuses on mine at every opportunity.

"Take your time. She should be stretched enough from recent activities to manage without too much trouble, but stop if she says so. We'll use the dilator if needed."

He says that like it's not ominous at all, and at my wide-eyed stare, he gestures to the tray where a metal halo-type contraption with a bundle of rods in the center sits. I'm shaking my head before he can even begin to explain. Just no. "Emmett, get it done. I'm not doing that."

Emmett's features are set with concern, but he doesn't hesitate to trail fingers through my nether lips, coating me liberally with the slick goop before slipping two inside to do the same to my vaginal walls. He retreats and picks up a long, loaded, blunt-tipped syringe before pushing it in to the hilt and emptying it inside.

The sensation of the lubricant hitting deep inside makes my muscles clench with a pang of arousal. I hadn't expected to like it, but that has been the case with most of what's gone on in this room. My body reacts to the stimulation regardless of whether the rest of me is on board. When he removes it, a bit trickles out, causing my cheeks to heat in embarrassment. It's not the most vulgar thing that's happened, or will happen, but some things are just hard to get used to.

"Alright, Wildcat, you ready?" I nod, briefly wondering if I should be completely flat. The slight incline lets me watch what's happening. I'm not sure if that's a good thing, but it makes me feel a bit more in control of the situation. "Tell me if it hurts," he orders as he pushes three fingers in.

It's a tight fit, but I know once I'm more loosened up, it'll be easy enough to add a fourth. It's the rest that I'm worried about as my memory reminds me of the women on the stage and those little hands plundering the holes presented to them.

Then Apollo joins in with a slender vibrator on my clit, the soft buzz the only warning before it hits the tip and makes me flex around Emmett's prodding digits. They keep at it until I'm flushing for a whole other reason, and when a small sound of pleasure escapes my throat, he adds that fourth finger and sinks in to his palm. With only the webbing where his thumb begins stopping his progress, he twists back and forth, spreading his fingers to make room for a bigger stretch before hooking them up into me to tease the sensitive spot that drives me crazy.

My moaning gasp is accompanied by my hips thrusting up in an effort to meet those wicked fingers curling inside, and I know I'll get off if he keeps on. But he doesn't. Instead, sketchy Angel boy retreats, the black glove shiny with both natural and synthetic fluids. Apollo obliges when Emmett holds his hand out and adds even more, making a small puddle in the palm of his cupped hand.

"Here goes, just relax as much as you can, okay?" Worry tinges Emmett's voice as his thumb tucks in to make the billed wedge that will open me wide.

Apollo clicks the vibrator off, and I want to demand it back on, but clenching is the opposite of what I'm supposed to do, so I settle back and do my best not to tense as the tips of all five digits hit my hole. Rapt fascination alternating with a terrifying dread, I watch as they disappear to the first knuckle.

The easy glide doesn't last as he presses forward. My skin grows taut, the edges trying to pull in, and he backs off on the pressure to try again, this time adding a slight twisting motion while advancing. I whimper as he passes the second set of knuckles, causing him to stop and glance up at me, his brows raised in question. At my nod, Emmett continues, and I bite my lip as I involuntarily tense from the pinch of pain.

Emmett's hand is nearly to the widest point, and while the sensation is overwhelming, it doesn't hurt terribly. But I'm feeling like that's about to change as things get more than snug. I start to panic when he stills, the pressure getting to be too much until Apollo coaches me through it.

"Bear down and breathe." My gaze flits to his, and he nods in encouragement. "It'll help, promise."

Taking him at his word, I take a deep breath, and as I let it out, I push out with my muscles while Emmett swivels his hand and squeezes in. My opening expands to allow him entry, and he pops in as a cross between a squeak and a grunt sounds in my throat. I'm lightheaded and nearly panting in relief when I see my hole close over his thick wrist.

Until Apollo brings the vibrator back and Emmett curls his fingers into a fist, rubbing the front wall of my pussy while giving a repeated pulsing clench. I'm overwhelmed with the odd feeling of extreme stretching and fullness. Even when Marcus and Brade had taken me together, I hadn't felt quite so stuffed, or maybe it was just in a different manner. Regardless, I begin to enjoy it, flexing my hips the small amount I dare with such a mass lodged inside me.

My eyes nearly cross when Emmett digs deep before pulling back to the full width of his fist, stopping with just his ridged knuckles holding the entrance of my pussy open so it strains obscenely until he relents at my whining protest and allows it to glide back in. He takes up an alternating rhythm of pushing and pulling with the occasional grind to my g-spot, eliciting nonstop soft sounds of pleasure accompanied by the wet noise of his motions and the buzz of the vibrator.

I come undone when Apollo removes the toy to lean in and capture my clit, sucking hard with flicks of his tongue. Emmett pulls back against my clamping pussy, gently shaking his fist with a moan of his own until I settle back as I come down from one of the hardest orgasms I've ever had.

Both men are heavy-lidded, arousal shining bright in their eyes, while I'm languid in the chair and considering a nap. But there's still the matter of getting Emmett's hand back out, and my still pulsating core isn't quite ready to let go. It doesn't help that Apollo is still lazily lapping at my clit, so I reach out to gently push him away. Mostly because I'm worn out and afraid to jostle the appendage in me too much.

After a few more moments to relax, Apollo directs Emmett to straighten his fingers and for me to bear down as Emmett carefully pulls out. The relief from the removal is short-lived and I wince at my complaining muscles worrying about how sore I'll be later. It's then that I notice the others have come close enough to watch, and if it wasn't for the twinge of refusal my pussy gives me at the thought, I'd take them up on their obvious interest.

(End of deleted scene)

21

GAME TIME

"**W**hy do I have to wear this? I look like a cosplay reject," I complain to Marcus about my outfit. He just gives me a bland look and gestures to himself and the holey metallic shirt and black leather pants. Okay, *maybe* we all have complaints.

"Come on, Birdie. You're rocking the warrior princess vibe." I roll my eyes at Braeden, trying to stay upbeat, but I still see the worry in his eyes.

Apollo strides into the bedroom, dressed much the same as Marcus. "We're as prepared as we can be. Remember, don't react or draw more attention than necessary." He pauses before delivering his last bit of news. "Our inside contact has disappeared. I took the chance on orchestrating for the video feed to the exhibition rooms to be cut off shortly after it begins. Robert won't want to alert the buyers that anything is amiss by announcing it. And I've sent a message to your handler." He indicates Rex and Emmett. "You all need immediate extraction. I gave him all the information I could send and hope they get here before anyone finds out. It's only a matter of *when*, not if, it's exposed."

If I wasn't afraid of being out of it, I'd ask for the drugs right about now. I was fucking petrified about our near future. Obviously, there was more to what had happened with Apollo and Marcus than they'd divulged.

Group somber, we all file to the outer door. Out of the corner of my vision I catch Apollo giving Marcus' shoulder an affectionate squeeze and a wry grin. Marcus catches me watching, expression resigned.

"It was a pipe dream to hope we'd make it out. Now our focus is on saving you five and as many other innocents as possible. And inflicting as much damage as we can before we're taken out." Marcus pushes up under my chin to close my mouth, dropping a peck on my lips as he walks past, then squaring his shoulders to face what's coming.

Braeden catches my attention, minutely motioning to our two martyrs. In silent commiseration, we agree they're coming with us too. *Won't they be surprised when they realize we won't let them sacrifice themselves?*

Walking into the exhibition room, it takes all I've got not to flip out or run right the hell back out. The guys are swallowing hard and averting their eyes too. Marcus and Brent trail a step behind and to Apollo's sides. They both hold leads to the leather cuffs binding my, Rex, Emmett, and Brade's hands in front of us. We make our way through the exhibits to our own area. The queening stool and pillories and such are one thing, but the piercing station, faux medical set-up, and a contraption resembling an iron maiden give me the shivers. Kitty corner to our spot is a black sheet covered object. *I don't even want to know.*

A nervous sweat gathers that not even an industrial strength antiperspirant is going to hinder. At least I'll have the excuse of exertion to cover it up soon. We arrive at our area and spread out to go over the positions of equipment and supplies and double check that there hasn't been any tampering. Brent managed to bring in an uncontaminated lubricant under the guise of me being extremely sensitive to the general dosed one that's used to keep the pets compliant. Technically, it's only supposed to be for me, and I'm to be drugged up by injection instead.

We spend a short time with last-minute instructions and are taking our places, along with the other occupants in the room, when Robert enters with an entourage.

A group of men and women head straight for our corner, making me tense up in worry. Several of the men are obviously guards, one in particular I'd prefer not to see again. As they get closer, one of the men is hooded and bound, being led by a guard.

Thankfully, for us, not so much the hooded man, they veer over to the covered contraption.

The big burly man is strapped to a saddle with a bit between his teeth and a halter on, the reins drawn up between his legs and crossed between his buttocks to hold them spread. His legs are bent and bound as well as his arms. His hood is pulled off and blinders put on with a screen in front of his face showing the framework behind him being directed at his ass. He's panicked and moaning.

Posted on the board for the exhibit is his crime, a guard caught trying out the merchandise and prolapsing a sold girl's anus before she was collected by her owner. The difference in price is being made up by auctioning him to the horse fetish buyers. Apparently their slaves don't last long, and this is his tryout to see if he can take it. I do a double take when I realize it's the man who was assaulting Emily in the janitor's closet. But she wasn't prolapsed when I helped clean her up. My face drains of blood as I realize she probably was abused further after Marcus and Apollo left her. I move away to find one of them and demand answers, but *he* comes in, and we're directed to watch. A case is opened, and Robert begins speaking.

"This was specifically made to size with a few embellishments. As you can see, it has a tube for the ejaculate. It's compared to a high-pressure hose when it empties. It also has three 'hooks'. Those are going to swell as the ejaculate is expelled before they're pulled out. Lubrication will be the liquid. A stallion only ruts for about two minutes before it's done, and there will be three rounds, so everyone has a chance to watch."

The horse dildo is pulled out and attached to the apparatus that will be doing the penetrating. We all watch with wide eyes as it's tested. It's eighteen inches long and three inches in diameter according to Robert. A tube is inserted into the man several inches, and Robert twists something at the base of the dildo to release the hooks. A four-leaf clover looking thing swells out of the tip to twice the width it already was, and the other end of the tube is hooked to it. Two more smaller bulges pop out along the shaft, and a bag is attached to the tube on the back of it.

Another twist and the man squeals around the bit. The tube had been inserted into the man's ass, and within seconds, the bag that contained at least a pint was sprayed into him. The tube is withdrawn from the anus, and lube leaks out, dripping to the floor. The dildo is reset, and more lubrication is rubbed over it. It's lined up with the man's ass, and now he's making unintelligible noises and trying to escape. Not that he can move an inch. I have a feeling this is going to do internal damage and think that's probably the point.

An example is being made out of him. I don't want to watch, but I'm afraid to look away with Robert observing. Robert addresses the small crowd once more. "The subject has been minimally stretched. The merchandise he damaged wasn't even given lubrication, so he should feel lucky. If he survives the night, the highest bid takes him to the farm." Robert finishes his speech, motioning for the guard doing the operating to begin.

The tip is lined up with the man's puckered hole, and the machine flipped on. Slowly but steadily, the machine forces the huge rod into the man's backside until the base is swallowed, and the metal arm follows it an inch or so into the gaping entrance. The man is staring at the screen in horror, now crying. His ass is going to be wrecked. The dildo is removed until the tip slips free, showing the tunnel-like hole left behind. A button is pushed, and a timer pops up. 120 seconds. Suddenly, the machine starts plunging hard and fast, ruthlessly impaling the man's ass. He's screaming around the bit, and the timer counts down. At ten seconds to go, it holds deep, and the man gets higher pitched. The hooks must have been released, and the bag begins emptying.

Lube is leaking around the metal rod, and then it starts to withdraw. The man is in a complete panic, and soon I can see why. The first ball passes and pulls on the abused hole. The second comes out larger, and now I can see flesh coming out along the shaft. With the third and final ball, several inches of bright pink insides builds up around a bulge trying to come out before the sphincter gives up, and it comes loose with a gush of fluid and a long, prolapsed tube of the man's ass.

The man passes out directly after, and I see some pink tint to the fluid coming out. Several of the patrons go up to fondle the extruding tissue and poke their fingers in it. Finally, the guard comes with a glove and slowly inserts it back into its cavity. You can tell it's hanging a little loose, and I doubt it will ever go back to what it was.

~

ROBERT CLAPS HIS HANDS SHARPLY, signaling for the exhibition to begin. While everyone had been preoccupied, several more of Robert's "guests" aka prospective buyers had come into the room. The set-up is much the same as the night on the stage had been. Servers for refreshments and pets to pass around.

Our group is third in the lineup with Robert doing his spiel about his son Apollo's special project. I'm not sure how much more I can stomach; muffled screams of pain and pleasure permeate the area. It's a hedonistic atmosphere that the sick fucks in charge are getting off on. *Literally*, in some cases.

22
PARTY CRASHERS

Stomach still churning from the display, Emmett and I take our places with the whips, beginning our sequence like pornographic carnival performers. We'd been nixed on going last as we would be too tired. I snap a paper straw from his mouth, garnering appreciative and interested looks from some of the men watching our part of the show.

Twitching my wrist to make the snake-like tail slither across the floor back to me in preparation for the next strike, I'm interrupted by a percussive booming coming from the entrance Robert had come through.

An air of disquiet runs through the crowd as the commotion continues. Robert has a phone out, lips moving swiftly, and thunder written across his face. Pausing, he glances up to our corner, zeroing in on Apollo. Death sits in his eyes. A shiver courses down my spine as he and his entourage of guards start moving our way. The guards are quickly engaged with other issues when an entrance opens up from a wall, allowing people covered head to toe in riot gear to swarm the room. Dull black helmets hide their identities, making it unclear whether they are friend or foe. Regardless, they have guns and are pointing them, demanding everyone get down.

Except for the people here that were patrons, and those that were able to move freely, they really can't comply as they're mostly bound. And the patrons and guards have zero intent on being detained. The resulting pops of discharging firearms echo in the space, nearly deafening. The group in gear is being more discriminating on who they are firing at; the bastards on the other side not so much, using human shields as needed.

I assume the armored people are some type of law enforcement by their actions, but they don't have any discernible markings, and Rex and Emmett aren't trying to get their attention. No, Rex is busy freeing the nearest bound slaves along with Brent while still protecting our corner as best they can.

Robert, seemingly ignoring the threat in his fury, is still on a path to get to Apollo. His screaming obscenities can be heard over the cacophony of the melee. He flips his jacket aside as he strides forward, the dull black glint more than clear in the light.

Apollo, of course, wasn't allowed a firearm since he was part of the entertainment.

Revenge and the urge to flee war within me. Brade yells for Emmett to get me back while he and Brent try to help Rex. Marcus had been helping clean up after the burly guard who had passed out and is fighting to get closer to my, or probably Apollo's, position.

It's all happening so fast that it's hard to take everything in. Escape doesn't seem a current possibility, so standing my ground is what is happening. Ignoring Emmett and Braeden, I zero in on Robert, who remains oblivious to my intent. As soon as he gets within reach, my whip snaps out, coiling around his throat.

Being a good deal larger than me doesn't matter when I

have surprise on my side. Twisting the length above the handle around my forearm I pull with both hands and feet planted, bringing him crashing down to the floor, unable to breathe or keep his grip on the gun he'd freed from its holster. It spins out of reach, and I take advantage of having the upper hand.

Shock registers on his face when he realizes what I've done. I start backing up to keep the coil taut, making Robert unable to get it loose.

Unfortunately, the invaders have different ideas about me ending the asshole. One of the helmeted bodies forcibly yanks the handle from me while another secures Robert's hands with zip ties.

A cry escapes me as my hand is wrenched, earning the interlopers Braeden and Emmett's immediate attention and ire.

While they're distracted, the guard that had caused me agony during the branding, also the one that still sports some yellowed bruises, decides to take his opportunity to get back at me. The impact of a fist to my cheek snaps my head back, pain blossoming immediately.

My disorientation allows them to cart me and a bound Robert off. Groggily, I hear a yell, then I'm dropped unceremoniously onto my bottom on the floor. I take in the scene, and even without it being directed towards me the sight is fearsome. Several more guards, more must have shown up from somewhere, and Apollo and Marcus are engaged in a full-on brawl. My guys aren't taking any prisoners. The snap of a neck takes a moment to place until the body hits the floor, limp with eyes staring sightlessly.

I'm shocked to find that Braeden is the culprit. His eyes full of ice and determination, he forces his way to my side.

"You okay, Birdie?" He grips on to my forearms, pulling me to my feet.

I start to nod my head yes when the throbbing in my face

reminds me not to make the motion. "Yes," I reply instead, cringing involuntarily. Braeden helps me further away from the fight, placing me behind a table.

The chaos is beginning to die down as the group in black gains control of the room's occupants. Some people have obviously fled as there seems to be a good deal less than there had been.

One person that *didn't* escape is Robert, who is being handcuffed, right along with Apollo and Marcus and the other still conscious guards.

Looking around the room, I find Rex, Emmett, and Brent all sitting against a wall, hands bound in front of them in a line of others. Everyone is being secured and detained, it seems.

Braeden tenses as a gun toting armored person comes toward us, motioning for our hands. A second person in black has a handful of zip ties, and a tinny masculine voice coming from a speaker on the helmet directs us to hold our wrists out together, and we're led to join the line on the wall

Mine aren't too tight, but I won't be easily slipping out of them either. I cause an issue when I try to check on Marcus who is now unconscious.

"Lark, he's fine. Just a tranq dart from a guard." Apollo is quick to reassure me when the demands for me to sit on the wall go unheeded, and tasers are brought out to force my compliance.

I relent, trusting Apollo to take care of him. I don't want Braeden, who is threatening to shove the taser up the man's ass, to get hurt.

The thought of Brade actually trying is rapidly becoming more amusing than I can handle, and a giggle escapes me. Clapping my bound hands to my mouth doesn't help, judging by range of expressions from the people that don't have helmets on. Peals of laughter sound out, slightly hysterical in manner.

"Fuck this." Brade, bound hands and all, tosses me over his shoulder, ignoring the group currently in charge to stalk to the wall.

I'm finally able to get myself under control. I bit my tongue on the way across the room, and the throbbing in my face has gotten my attention. Then I realize my warrior princess ass is on full display in the faux leather briefs I have on, and I'm really ready to get down.

Finally settled, I tip my head on Braeden's shoulder. "Sorry, I lost it there for a minute."

In reply, he rests his on top of mine. We've sat this way many times over the years. Well, minus the cuffs, among other things.

"No talking. And separate." The gruff command comes from one of the helmets.

Stifling an eye roll, I comply. Hopefully, they hurry up with whatever they're doing. I'm ready for regular clothes and to get away from this nightmare. My not-so-terrified attitude is also making me think that rat ass Marcus slipped me something despite my refusal. Or I'm in shock— that's probably more plausible.

Turns out they really are law enforcement, a joint special forces team sent in when Apollo called for help. The liaison that went MIA was found dead in his apartment, spurring the immediate action to bust in. While a few of the trafficking ring escaped, it's still a win to shut it down.

We're eventually all moved to the upper levels and separated into groups to be processed at an FBI facility in the area. Several hours, a never-ending interview, and many hoops of procedure to deal with later, we're all in multi-person rooms with bunks for temporary holding, or, in the case of victims who'd been held for years or from out of the country, much longer. I don't know what is happening with the guys as I haven't been able to talk to them since the initial separation when we left the spa. I tried asking, but no one would give me any answers.

23

I HAVE RIGHTS, ASSHOLE

aking after a fitful night's rest, I'm arguing with my assigned doctor and nurse that I won't submit to more than a general exam. They're trying to insist on a full panel of bloodwork and a rape kit. I refuse, explaining I'd rather go to my own doctor after I get home.

"Miss Jones, it's protocol in this situation to perform a full battery of tests." The middle-aged pleasant looking female doctor is losing patience after being called in by the nursing staff when I declined— repeatedly— to get into a gown or let them draw blood.

"I don't give a rat's ass what your protocol is. I'm an American citizen with rights. One of those rights is to make my own medical decisions unless I've been deemed incompetent by a judge. If you *don't* have the document stating that, then I suggest you discharge me."

The doctor walks out, trailed by the nurse, lips pursed in disapproval.

I take the chance to walk out and find someone in charge that can tell me exactly why I'm not being let go. I'm a goddamned *victim* not a fucking criminal. Which is what I scream at the guard who tries to block me from leaving the medical facility— right before I cold-cock him and drop him on his ass for touching me.

"Well, I guess it was true when I was told you're a scrappy little hellcat that can hold her own." I whirl at the masculine voice behind me, prepared to further defend myself if necessary. "I come in peace— but please tell me it's true you actually threw batteries and smacked folks around with a whip. The reports coming across my desk are gruesome, and your shenanigans have at least been some comic relief in the sad story that is the Vitti empire.

Done with Mr. Suave and Disarming— who apparently knows a lot more about me than I do him— I carefully edge my way until my back is against the hallway wall, and I don't have to take my eyes off him or the dazed guard.

"I'd say it's nice to meet you, except it's not, and you haven't bothered to introduce yourself. Kindly, go fuck yourself— I'm leaving."

Mr. Suave chuckles, but his joviality isn't hiding the shrewdness in his dark eyes. His salt and pepper hair and slight paunch won't make me hesitate to smack him if he touches me. I've had *enough* of being touched.

"Please, excuse my rudeness, I'm Assistant Director Chappel of the FBI, ma'am. If I could just take a moment of your time to get a signature, I can get you on your way real quick like." He aims what he probably thinks is a disarming smile at me.

Fuck you, buddy.

"If it's all the same to you, I'd rather not. Feel free to mail it and I'll return it. Buh-bye now." It's unsurprising when I don't get very far, but hey, it was worth a shot.

He finally drops the good ole' boy routine, letting some steel enter his tone. "Miss Jones, I'm going to have to insist. If you'd please accompany me. Or I can call for assistance as you're obviously still under some strain. Maybe a sedative and some more rest would be beneficial—"

I cut him off. "You son of a bitch. I fucking *dare* you. I'll have your ass slapped with lawsuits from now until the next decade, and it's self-defense if I damage any of your 'personnel'. Get me someone I know. Preferably, three someones, and I'm sure you can figure out who they are considering you're the big man on campus." I take a breath and continue my tirade. "Not one person has bothered to give me *any* information. Not even the fucking date. I was kept in captivity with a very loose sense of time. I'd imagine it's a weekday with all the personnel swarming over this place, except it's got to be the bust of your career, and I'm sure it's all hands on deck."

I'm unsure what exactly my rights are in this situation, but they can't just hold me indefinitely while treating me like a damn criminal lab rat.

Seeming to relent, the man reaches for a radio clipped to a belt under his jacket. "Get me Agents Baelor and Lancer in my office immediately, please. Oh, and send someone to assist the guard at the East exit in the medical ward." A voice responds in the affirmative, and the Assistant Director clips the radio back in its place. Offering his arm with a "Walk with me?" he waits expectantly.

I decline the arm, but walk toward him until we're even with as much of the hall between us as I can get. I follow him down the corridor and past the nurses' station where the disapproving doctor and nurse stand watching with matching lemon sucking expressions. Bet the bitches tattled on me. I flip them off before we pass through the double doors into another corridor.

"Well, now, that wasn't polite."

"You really going tell me they *didn't* report me for being

uncooperative?" His non answer is all I need for confirmation. "Thought so."

AFTER A FEW MORE TURNS THROUGH cloned hallways, we finally stop at a door. Upon entering, I find myself in a reception room with Rex and Emmett standing at the secretary's desk. Emmett is watching the door while Rex appears to be chatting up the secretary.

Before the Assistant Director can stop me, I launch myself at Emmett. His arms are open before I even make it to him, and he scoops me up in a bear hug.

"Fuck, hellcat. They said you were okay, but it's good to see you in the flesh." I don't get a chance to ask for an explanation since the Assistant Director demands us to separate.

"Agent Lancer, if you would please remove yourself from Miss Jones, it would be much appreciated." Phrased prettily but not really a request.

Emmett reluctantly lets me go, and I move back to keep the empty corner of the room behind me. I ask my next question— well, demand is more like it.

"Where's Braeden?" Rex looks guilty. So does Emmett. I panic and yell at the Assistant Director, "Where the fuck is he?"

"Lark, baby, calm—"

"Miss Jones, in my office." Rex and his apparent boss speak at the same time.

I stomp past them and the wide-eyed secretary at the desk to push my way into a room through the only other door available. I ignore the decor besides the fact that it has a window, chairs, and a desk. Whirling to wait impatiently, I stand with my back against the window.

The men don't dawdle, but they're not moving fast enough

to suit my panic. Thankfully, the AD doesn't make me wait long.

"Miss Jones, would you like a seat?" I shake my head no and he continues. "Braeden Bancroft was released to go home this morning. He put up a fuss about waiting on you, but as we are overtaxed at the moment, we had to insist he do his waiting at home. Agents Baelor and Lancer have been busy themselves with debriefing and routine medical tests. The same tests you just refused, and we still have your debriefing to handle."

I don't understand. Not a fucking bit of it. If the guys were obviously taken care of last night and at the butt crack of dawn, why am I still here? I voice my concerns out loud, earning surreptitious glances from them that don't include me.

"Fucking spit it out. I'm sick of this shit. I haven't done anything wrong, and you're keeping me here."

I'm apparently wearing on the AD's patience. "Miss Jones, I'm going to have to insist that you calm down."

Rex agrees with him— the dick— while Emmett looks torn and confused as well. I just want *someone* to explain things.

"Miss Jones, I'm going to bring in an agent to record your statement and female Special Agent Medic to catalogue any physical records."

The brand. Son of a bitch. That's what the nosey ass females wanted earlier.

I'm evidence.

The AD steps out to speak with his secretary, giving me a chance to talk to the men I'm really having some trust issues with at the moment.

"What the hell, Rex? Why am I getting the special treatment? It's as straightforward as you two and Brade. Or isn't it?"

"Lark, I'm sorry, but I'm not at liberty to discuss an ongoing investigation." His expression is shuttered, and I feel the last corner of my heart that held affection for him crumble with his words.

"You knew— you fucking knew this would happen, didn't you?" He doesn't answer, and Emmett looks pained. "Fuck you, both. You let this happen. This is *your fault, Rex!* Get. Out. I don't want to see either of you again." I'm so raw emotionally it's taking everything I have not to collapse in a blubbering heap.

"Lark, please—" Emmett beseeches me.

I turn my back on them, waiting until I hear the door open and close again. Sinking into one of the chairs, I sit until a knock precedes the door opening.

"Miss Jones, if you could come with me, please," a dark-haired man close to my age with a crossbody bag on beckons from the open doorway.

I get up from the chair, moving in a fog of surreality to the reception room. To find the AD speaking in hushed tones with Emmett, and Rex leaning over the desk chatting up the secretary. Rex and the woman look up as I pass in time to catch my scathing glare.

Like his dick hasn't had enough action for a month at least.

Emmett doesn't even attempt to look at me. I put my head down and follow the agent down the hall to a conference room and settle into a chair at the table.

He introduces himself, but I'm not really paying attention. I'm just done at this point. I do vaguely hear him say he's going to record the session, and he asks me to sign paperwork to that effect. I try to decline signing anything as I'm in no condition to be doing so, but I get the spiel about being stuck here until I comply.

While I'm attempting to explain I'm not randomly signing anything, a woman comes in the room carrying a large case. She lays it out on the other end of the table and begins taking equipment out. A camera, blood draw supplies, a gown and blue chuck pads, and the list goes on. She goes to a door at the other end of the room I hadn't noticed when I came in. She comes back out and disappears into the hall.

The agent is trying to direct my attention back to the papers he wants me to sign when some intuition is telling me to go investigate what's behind that open door.

Despite the man's protests, I get up and walk over to it. It's nearly deja vu. An exam table— complete with stirrups folded in their little cubbies— sits in the middle of the room. Horror overtakes me as I retreat back into the conference room. The woman has returned, carrying another case.

Intent on her mission, she grabs a few of the supplies off the table and enters the room I can still see into. She sets the case on a counter and repeats the laying out of items onto a surgical tray. The usual things needed for a full female exam.

Fuck. This.

I grab the papers off the table and start skimming past all the legal mumbo-jumbo crap. On the second page I find what I'm looking for. Consent to a full debriefing and subsequent physical examination. I jerk my head up to glare at the agent.

"Do you know what these papers say? Of course, you do. And you're sitting here trying to badger me into signing them. Go fuck yourself." I rip the packet into quarters despite both personnel protesting.

I dart out the door and go back to the hall I think I remember the AD's office being in. I find the plaque and storm in right past the surprised secretary and into the AD's room.

Rex and Emmett. Hadn't counted on them still being here.

"You piece of shit. I'm a victim that was pulled into your bullshit operation by your incompetent agent. I want a lawyer. You're not doing jack shit to me without one *and* a warrant." I turn my fury on the men I'd thought I could trust. "Is Braeden even at home? Did you two consent to an invasive internal exam? Did he get badgered into signing his consent away? How about hopping yourself back up into a lovely exam chair?"

They both pale at my questions, turning to look at their boss. "It's SOP in these cases. She had a lot more interaction and chances at verifying the informants' story. She was alone with them."

Emmett replies to the AD's explanation. "With all due respect, Assistant Director, what you're requesting her to do isn't standard operating procedure for traumatized victims. I don't know what is going on here, but Lark doesn't know anymore than we've already told you. And you're well aware of her treatment—"

The AD interrupts him, "Agent Lancer, you're excused. No, not another word."

Emmett stalks out of the room. Rex has a frown between his brows but holds his tongue— for once.

"Miss Jones, if you don't consent, we can't do our jobs, and you'll be staying indefinitely. Would you like Agent Baelor to be present? It's not quite protocol, but if it would make you more comfortable, I think we can work something out. What do you say, Agent? You're up for helping a witness, aren't you? One that was victimized when protocol wasn't followed?"

Is this smarmy motherfucker really blackmailing us into doing what he wants? My jaw about hits the floor when Rex gives a sharp nod without even inquiring about my wishes.

"While Rex may be willing— I'm not. I wasn't bluffing when I asked for an attorney. And if Braeden is still here, I'll be requesting one for him as well. We both have emergency power of attorney paperwork filed with his business attorney, and I'm pretty sure this could count as emergent."

The AD loses his cool, and I'm actually scared he's going to hit me. Rex still has some sense because he tries to intervene. Thankfully, he doesn't need to as the intercom comes on.

"Assistant Director Chappel, I'm sorry to interrupt, but I have a Mr. Bancroft here with an attorney demanding the release of Miss Lark Jones. He has paperwork from a local judge to support his demands."

I close my eyes in thanks that my ride or die bestie came through. I don't waste any time escaping. I'm still dressed in the gray scrub-like outfit and house shoes I'd been given last night when we arrived—and I don't care a bit. I'm fucking going home.

24

GOING HOME

Emmett asks and is granted permission to escort me out. He keeps ahold of my arm the entire way despite my animosity toward him. I pick up the pace, dragging him with me when I spot Braeden waiting on me at the exit.

The person I'm presuming to be the attorney— and I could kiss the man right now— puts a staying arm out to stop Brade from meeting me when the guards next to the metal detector get antsy.

We walk through it moments later, and I'm in Brade's arms instantly. He picks up his head to peer at Emmett over my shoulder.

"Thanks man," he whispers.

"Not a problem, just doing my job." I don't understand, but I don't care. I'm free.

We exit the building, and I look back once, to see Emmett and Rex, side by side, with matching sorrowful countenances. That's all I allow, and then I shut the door on this chapter in my life. I'm sure I'll have to answer questions at some point, but it's not now, and for that I'm grateful.

Arriving home several hours later, I head straight for the shower. Where I break down in uncontrollable sobs. Braeden finds me sometime later once the water has run cold, and I'm shivering and blue.

"Birdie, no." He yanks me out, shutting the water off, wrapping me in a towel, and heading straight for my bed, uncaring about the water trailing from me.

Under the blankets, he strips to his boxers, wrapping me in his body heat. My teeth chattering, I stutter out an apology.

"I'm so sorry, Brade. It's all too much. And I don't know what you had to do to get released. That man is a monster."

"Lark, honey, all I did was give a quick statement that corroborated the other guys, general blood work and a urine test, and let them take a picture of the brand. That's it. I didn't even have to get undressed further than exposing my underwear. They even offered to let me have it done at my own doctor's office to check if I picked anything up while we were there, which didn't matter to me either way. I don't know what they were after with you. Emmett facilitated my release and told me to get you an attorney immediately."

"Wait, what? Emmett? But he— Oh, no." I feel like an ass after I treated him like shit. "Did Rex—?" I don't know how to finish that.

"No, pretty bird. Just Emmett." It's nice to have someone that can interpret your thoughts when you can't voice them.

"Brade, I think I'm gonna need to talk with someone." He just hugs me tighter.

"I know. I'll be going too. It's already being set up."

I drift off, knowing he'll be there for me, no matter what.

~

Six Weeks Later

I've GONE to several appointments with an FBI approved counselor and had a general, non-invasive work up done with my own medical provider. The doctor cleared me, but the counselor has me taking anti-anxiety meds to keep the panic attacks at bay.

I haven't seen nor heard from Rex or Emmett and have only found out about Marcus and Apollo from what's been on the news. Brade usually shuts it off when he catches me watching it. Thankfully, our address hasn't been leaked to the media yet, and we both can stay home for awhile longer with our savings.

Braeden and I still haven't discussed anything relationship-wise other than we're still as close as ever. Maybe with time, that'll be a topic, but right now I'm just too confused. The meds seem to be helping lessen the panic attacks that were beginning to take over. The official diagnosis: PTSD. *No shit, people.*

Except I'm not sure how much longer I can take them as I stare at the little stick that is currently rocking my world. Two. Fucking. Pink. Lines.

This isn't happening.

I'M TRYING to keep my shit together when Braeden starts banging on my bedroom door. "Lark!" The panic in his voice prompts me to stash the test in the drawer under the sink and exit my ensuite bathroom.

I find Braeden harried and rushing around my room, throwing clothes in a duffel bag. "Get your toiletries, we have to go. Now, Lark!"

"Brade, calm down and tell me what's happening."

A voice I wasn't sure I'd hear again answers me instead.

"Lark, move your ass. Pops escaped and is out for blood. Grab your stuff and let's go." It's Marcus, using my actual name, with Apollo standing directly behind him.

I give a happy cry and hug first Marcus and then Apollo. "How did you guys get here?" I hadn't realized how worried I've been about them.

"Please, Nightingale, there's no time. We have to hurry. My father could be watching your house, I'll explain on the way." I nod and start to help Braeden.

"Birdie, I got the clothes and shoes, but if you want tampons, you'd better get them now." The reminder causes me to feel faint.

Oh, fuck.

CONTINUE READING FOR A SNEAK
PEEK OF NIGHTINGALE

Two Flew the Coop

Oh, fuck. Oh, fuck. Oh, fuck. Oh, fuck. What do I do now?

I'm so scrambled at the urgency and the reunion that I'm not sure what I'm even grabbing for toiletries. My bag is filling up rapidly; so hopefully, I'm taking what I need. My mind is firmly on the stick I hid in my bra.

Fucking nosey ass FBI and psychotic criminals make it where I doubt even my trash is safe. I even flushed the packaging. Well, tried to anyway. Currently, a piece of the box is trying to make a comeback, but it's not like I can get away with plunging it with Braeden right on the other side of the door–he'd insist on coming in to fix it.

So, pee stick in the bra it is, and a closed toilet lid with a prayer that it all disintegrates into an unrecognizable pulp. At least the wrapper actually made it down. I'll have to find somewhere along the way to ditch the test.

Bag full, I'm heading for the door when the boxes of tampons and pads on the shelf above the toilet catch my eye. *Can't forget those after Brade's comment.*

Stuffing them in the bag, I take a deep breath, gather my composure, and exit the bathroom.

I find Apollo is the only one waiting for me, with two bags resting at his feet, while he peruses the collage frames on the wall.

The pictures are from all my big moments as well as having the last one taken of my parents before they died in a car crash a couple of years ago.

Coming up behind him, I tentatively address Apollo. "I think I'm all finished if you're ready."

He spins, features unreadable except his piercing eyes. Without warning, he scoops me up, crushing my chest to his, and fuses our lips roughly. His tongue doesn't waste any time demanding entry, and I acquiesce immediately, twining my arms around his neck to keep him there.

Right or wrong, some fucked up mental thing or not, he became more important than I'd thought. Both of them, actually. I hadn't realized just how dearly I'd missed him and Marcus. The adjustment to coming home has been so jumbled and emotional that I'd avoided my feelings on the subject. Even in therapy, which I know I shouldn't, but I just couldn't deal with judgment or being told I'm wrong in my feelings.

A throat clearing interrupts the moment, and Apollo slowly lowers me until my feet reach the floor. The intense eye contact he holds as he does so makes it clear that we'll be finishing this later.

"Alright, you two. Time to go, suck face later. And Birdie, thank fuck, that's the first I've seen that things are going to be okay." Braeden has a half-smile on his face when I turn in Apollo's embrace to look at him.

"Been having issues, Nightingale?" Apollo tips his head down to whisper in my ear.

Uncomfortable, I shrug and move away. *Who wouldn't have issues? Even Brade has had some bad days.*

"A few, but it's getting better." I aim a death glare at my bestie when he starts to open his mouth. Marcus, standing in the doorway behind him, cocks a brow in surprise but stays quiet on the subject.

"If we have everything, let's get going. I don't want to chance any mishaps, so we'll meet up with the others as soon as we can," Marcus says.

"Wait, I thought we were going to separate safe houses." Apollo's confusion is apparent.

Marcus waves us along to get moving. "We were, but Brent's was hit, along with a couple of others. Now Rex and Emmett have gone for him, and we're going to one of my bug-out set-ups. They're looking for us, and from what I've pieced together, they're after Lark to draw you out. We, or rather *you*, didn't hide your feelings very well." Marcus' explanation is worrisome, to say the least.

With a last look around to check for anything I'll need, I step out the back door, Braeden locking up behind us. A black SUV with darkly tinted windows is idling next to our rear gate in the alley. We stow our bags in the cargo area and hop in the back, leaving Marcus and Apollo the front seats. Apollo takes shotgun while Marcus gets behind the wheel.

Apollo has a tablet out with a Bluetooth headset hooked up to it. Marcus catches my questioning glance in the mirror and explains, "He's watching the reports and listening for any chatter that indicates where Robert is now." I get the drift that it's not exactly legal, but I don't comment on it.

Marcus is checking and double-checking every intersection before he crosses through it, and it's got my anxiety ramped up something awful. The feeling has me pushed directly back into the mindset of not being taken again, and I keep my thoughts to myself, knowing no one in the vehicle would appreciate them. *Me or them, that shit ain't happening a second time.*

Once we've made it a ways out of the city, Marcus relaxes

his vigilance slightly. Frankly, with it being nearly dark and mostly open space, it would be hard not to see someone coming. He must deem it safe enough to explain more and gives us vague information on where we're going.

"Apollo has had me set up places near to everywhere we've been over the years. In the event something ever happened to him, or that I, or both of us, ever needed to run, there are set-ups all over the world with full contingency plans."

At least we should be safe. Hopefully, Robert is taken out or re-captured quickly. I have my own issues, big and small, to deal with, and unfortunately, one of them is fairly time-sensitive. I can't indefinitely hide out without anyone finding out. The itchy plastic feels like it's fused to my skin inside my bra, a constant reminder that I'm massively screwed.

Thinking of Robert or the test gives me a panicky sensation, and I try to suppress it. The panic attacks are getting better, but the news that Robert escaped is petrifying. The asshole who ran The Facility, a sex-trafficking ring hidden under a legitimate spa, is responsible for all the bad things in my recent past *and* my current predicaments. It's not going to be pleasant if he catches any of us on the run with Apollo. He's already abused his son for his entire life and Marcus' as well. I mean, who buys a child sex slave for their own kid and gives him as a present after killing said kid's mom and brother?

Robert Vitti, that's who. He also facilitated the branding scars we all share now, well, minus Apollo. As the heir to the shady empire, he got a tattoo of the symbol, a little sun with wavy rays extending from it— I shudder at the thought of it. I've been violated enough on the elder Vitti's orders and have zero intentions of meeting up with him again. I am at least happy to see Apollo and Marcus doing well; they were brave and good men helping to bring Robert down at the risk of their own lives— even if their methods were sometimes cruel.

Settling further into my seat, I try to blot out the memories.

Brade will hound me for a week if he thinks I need his assistance— whether I want it or not.

My beautiful olive-toned bestie is always my happy place, but he can be overprotective sometimes. I mean, I can't really blame him after my d-bag of an ex dragged us both into the mess to begin with. Rex dumping me was only the start of a very bad evening. The revelations about his job and Emmett, his partner, were eye-opening to say the least. Briefly, I wonder what the sketchy angelboy is doing.

Then I mentally smack myself. I need to chill and figure things out, not dwell on the past that can't be changed or the assholes who got me into the mess in the first place. Mind made up to relax as long as I can, my attention turns back to the scenery passing outside the tinted windows.

We turn off the main road to go onto a narrower lane leading up into the foothills of a small mountain range. We've been driving for hours, and I need to pee, but I don't really want to get out and squat unless I have to. I'd thought there would have been at least one stop, but that hasn't happened, which means I'm still hiding this damn stick.

More turns and a steady incline into the forested area and I'm beginning to get lost. We've left the paved roads and have gone from graveled to mostly dirt, narrow, one-lane tracks. *Where the hell are we going?*

Finally, when my bladder is near to bursting, we crest the top of a hill to find a decidedly *un*-rustic, two-story, cabin on a plateau, illuminated by floodlights on poles. It suits its surroundings rather well despite its size, done in large half-rounds of timbered trees and chinked together. I can even see two separate bricked chimneys poking up out of the roof. What I'm not seeing though are power lines. Looking around, I notice squares of flat black mounted on the poles, and upon closer inspection, larger ones on the roof of the cabin.

It's all solar-powered. Huh, didn't expect that. Or to be going off-grid.

The SUV rolls to a stop after we drive around to a carport behind the cabin, and I can see a covered porch running the length of the back of it. I've gone to pull my handle, as peeing has become rather urgent, when Marcus halts me.

"Let me check it out first. I haven't been up here in a while and need to clear it." He must catch my panicked glare because he adds on that he'll hurry. "Five minutes, there's no reason to believe anyone is here, just being safe."

Braeden guesses my predicament as I flop back in my seat while Apollo moves to get behind the wheel, where he proceeds to back the vehicle into the carport. "Need to pee, Birdie?"

"Nah, I'm crossing my legs and doing the potty dance for your amusement." I roll my eyes at him then widen them in incredulity as he gets out, walks around the edge of the carport wall, and blatantly whips it out to urinate. I mean, I can't see the stream, but that stance pretty much says it all. "Fuck you, Brade. I hope a forest bug bites it off!" I can hear his chuckle through the open door, and even Apollo lets out a soft chuff.

"Good thing you're all so quiet and watchful, huh?" I screech, nearly losing control of my bladder as Marcus scares the bejesus out of me. Which of course just makes the other two laugh harder.

"Marcus, I swear to fuck, if you don't get me to a toilet in the next sixty seconds, you're cleaning the seat." Not that I'd actually pee in the car, but it's a good threat and gets him moving.

"Apollo, you and Braeden okay to get the bags?" At a nod from both, he hot-foots me inside using the backdoor.

We get through a basic laundry room and short hall, and I

barely register the minimal yet tasteful decor as he points to a door right off the living room we came out into. I ensconce myself inside, and drop onto the toilet, barely getting my pants down as my butt makes contact with the wooden seat. A minute or two later, with a sore but empty bladder, I get my pants up and hands washed. Ignoring my reflection, I exit the bathroom to find the guys dragging the luggage in.

"So, where are the others?" I'm curious as to why Rex, Emmett, and Brent aren't here yet.

Marcus answers, "I'm trying to find out now. We came to get you while they went after Brent." Marcus has a phone out, and I'm wondering how he has service. He must notice my confusion. "We're high enough up that we're picking up a signal; we only lose it on the lower roads. And I'm going to have to go get them. Their truck was hit, and the authorities have the attackers, but they can't get a new vehicle under the radar at this point."

"Are they okay?" I demand.

"Yes, they're fine, minus some bumps and bruises. The airbags went off, or they'd have continued on. Apollo, you can get them settled and everything without me, right?" Marcus is already heading for the front door as he answers my question, and I wonder why he didn't bring me in that way. *Maybe he forgot the bathroom was closer to it?*

Apollo nods while I'm still pondering the inanity, waving Marcus off when he pauses with the door ajar. "I can handle pointing things out. Go on, and be safe. I expect a call or message when you pick them up and again before you lose cell service." Marcus agrees, shutting the door behind him as he leaves. "Upstairs or down? Bunking together or separate rooms?"

I'm faintly shocked that Apollo would ask if I want to share with Braeden, but then again, he might assume we're together. It's not as if we've talked since we were carted off in different directions that day. I glance up the stairwell, trying to decide.

I must take too long to answer, as Brade says, "Separate is fine, right, Birdie?"

"Yes, that's fine with me. Sorry, I think I'm still a bit off, with all the events today. And upstairs or down doesn't matter. I would just like to be next to Braeden if that's possible." I may not feel the need for a slumber party, but I still want to keep him close.

"Up it is then. There are two of the smaller bedrooms that share a bathroom. I believe the previous owners used them for children."

I nearly choke on my spit at Apollo's mention of children. The damn test feels like a brand against my skin. Wait, scratch that, maybe a neon sign. Fuck, I've avoided that brand, seeing or touching it, like the plague since we got home. Today has just got me all out of sorts. Apollo gives me a strange look, and I hope my guilt isn't written all over my face. For all I know, he *could* be the baby daddy. Jesus, fuck. Baby. Daddy. Two words I didn't need in my immediate vocabulary.

I shake off my weirdness before Brade starts asking questions and heft the overnight bag I threw my toiletries in onto my shoulder, but Apollo grabs the suitcase Brade packed for me and heads for the stairwell on the wall that divides the living room from the kitchen.

Apollo gives commentary as he leads us up the carpeted steps. "There's the main level with all the usual rooms, master bedroom, guest bedroom, two bathrooms, an office, and a security room. The security room is locked as is my office. There's a sublevel--" I give an involuntary shudder at that and even notice Brade stiffening out of the corner of my eye. "It's locked as well, there is no reason either of you would need to go down there. Well, I suppose the breaker box and batteries and safe room are down there, but that's worst-case scenario, and Marcus or I can handle the power if that issue arises."

I'm still curious about the way the solar power works but finding out it's in the basement quells my intent to explore that interest. Apollo is silent until we reach the landing, and it's highly uncomfortable.

He sighs before he starts again. "I apologize for not getting you out sooner; it was never my intent to drag any more innocents into that atrocity. I hope someday you can forgive me for my part in your trauma."

Dropping my bag and closing the distance to Apollo, I hug him tight, and after a brief hesitation, his arms come around me. "Wasn't really your fault, so there's nothing to forgive. I'm a tiny bit buggered up, but I'm working through it. The bestie--" I tip my head in Braeden's direction, "has been helping a lot." Stepping back, Apollo almost reluctantly lets go, and I gesture in both directions the landing splits into. "Which way?"

Apollo leads us to the left branch, and I pick up my bag to follow him. Brade elbows me as I pass him, giving me a smirk and a wink when I shoot him a glare. The brat is game for *anything* to help cheer me up. I suppose now I'll be facing my demons head-on. With that worrying thought, I follow Apollo into a cheery yellow bedroom. A queen-sized bed with a night-stand, dresser, and a recliner in the corner next to it is the only furniture in the room.

"The other room is the same, but in green. The furniture and bedding are new." Apollo seems a bit bashful about the colors. "The bathroom is through that door, and there's a small closet through here." He opens a door showing an inset with a shelf and rod in it, stowing my suitcase on the carpeted floor. Small but serviceable.

I drop my overnight bag on the foot of the bed before crossing to the bathroom door to peek in; it's all done in plants. Yellow and green plants. Now I see where he may have been embarrassed about not updating the decor. I shrug, not really caring about the design or color scheme. At this point, a bed is a bed as long as it's safe. Walking through past the double sink and tub/shower combo, I open the other door and continue into a mirror image of my room, but in pastel green.

Brade walks in to drop his own bags while Apollo exits out the hallway door. "We'll be okay here, Birdie. Surely, they know what they're doing. Let's go see what they have for dinner. If I'm starving, I know you are. Plus, you need to take your meds." I stay still as Brade leaves the room, trying to figure out how to avoid taking my medication. It's not like I got the chance to consult an OB. Braeden pauses outside the door, blatantly waiting for me. He's been doing that a lot lately, refusing to leave me alone.

ABOUT THE AUTHOR

Emma Cole is a multi-genre romance author covering everything from dark and light contemporary to paranormal and sci-fi. Almost all of her stories are, or will be, from the reverse harem subcategory, and none of them skimp on the heat.
Emma lives in the mountains in the Northwest U.S with her kiddos and fur babies where she only puts on 'town pants' when absolutely necessary.

∽

Follow Emma

Newsletter Sign-Up
https://www.subscribepage.com/emmacole

Reader Group
Emma's Author Stalkers

ALSO BY EMMA COLE

DARK REVERSE HAREM BOOKS

Bad Habits Duology

No Good Deed

No Bad Deed

Twisted Love Series

The Degradation of Shelby Ann

Dark Duet

Lark

Nightingale

COLLEGE CONTEMPORARY REVERSE HAREM

Remington Carter Series

Echoes

Requiem

Clarity

DARK PARANORMAL REVERSE HAREM

Blackbriar Academy

The Order: Hit and Run

The Order: Ascension

Order of the Wraith

Avarice: House of Mustelid (Wicked Reform School)

SCI-FI/ALIEN ROM-COM

Alie and the Cosmic Convicts (standalone)

Printed in Great Britain
by Amazon